Sound Distortion

A Novel by Kurt Gailey

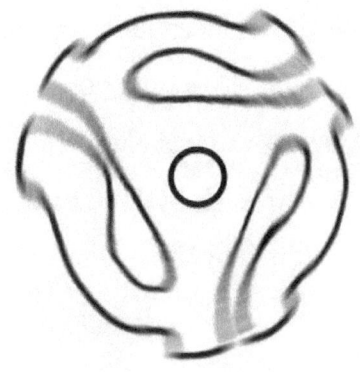

Published by Glass Spider Publishing

www.glassspiderpublishing.com

ISBN 978-0-9997070-4-3

Library of Congress Control Number: 2018934027

Cover design by Jane Font

Edited by Vince Font

 GLASSSPIDERPUBLISHING

This one's for Jon, Johnny, John, Johan, Ian, Ivan, Sione, Jane, Johnette, Joan, and Janet.

Acknowledgments

A huge thanks is due to Vince Font and everyone else at Glass Spider Publishing. What are the chances that so many professionals would manage to congregate in one place? I think the chances are slim, and yet it happened. From the editing to the video production, every aspect of publication is mastered by someone at Glass Spider Publishing. Thank you all.

Table of Contents

1. Mutating Facility 9

2. See the Seeler Seethe 15

3. How to Play Baseball on the Subway 19

4. The Execution of the Ambient 23

5. Aphrodisiac Jacket 28

6. How Did Anyone Get Angry Before Heavy Metal? 34

7. If You Can't Sing, SCREAM!! 37

8. No Coffee Mug 43

9. Song Ten is Missing? 48

11. Ten Fingers to Burn 52

12. In the Absence of Heat 58

13. Break Down 64

14. Fork, Spork, Splork 69

15. Pop Rocks? Are You Sure? 73

16. Unwind, Rewind 81

17. Everybody Wants 84

18. The Rich Man Keeps What the Poor Man Throws Away 88

19. Change Your Name to Fit the Band 91

20. Staring Down the Grooves of a 45 98

21. If You're Foxy, I'm Comin' to Get Ya 104

22. Blades in Stereo 111

23. Once Upon a Fish 119

10. The Sirkus (Epilog) 124

1. Mutating Facility

Every teenager enjoys seeing and hearing a little distortion now and again. Once within that age group, a person will come to the turning point in life in which they recognize the general reality—and a possible escape from it.

Downtown 34th Street was the favorite place for many children Djonny's age when they were skipping school. The street was a dedicated tech haven, and all of the shop owners had long ago converted their storefronts to hologram façades.

There were certain moments during the year when all of the storefronts would change at once in preparation for upcoming calendar events. If a viewer was there at one of those times, he or she could watch the street transform from a lifelike vista of Sydney, Australia, in 1963 to El Paso, Texas, in 1888—or from Salt Lake City's Temple Square at Christmas to the United Arab Emirates' Dubai Bazaar.

When these transformations took place, the entire street became a magical, flickering wonderland. Always between the two scenes there was a third, and a person had to watch very closely to catch it because it only became visible for half a second. This momentary vision was the real street, where hologram panels covered every building. Only the doors and windows had no panels, but images were cast onto them by projector. All of 34th Street was an ultra-clean environment in comparison to the rest of the dingy city; if projection panels got the least bit dirty, glitches would mar the hologram images.

Djonny was there on the day the scene changed from a wild Martian landscape to a spooky series of haunted houses and bewitched castles. In preparation for Hallowe'en, 34th Street had been electronically shapeshifted to a setting where the cursed buildings cowered in perpetual night. Djonny still had the brightly-chromed, other-worldly landscape burned into his retinas when the transformation took place, and for a brief moment it created an odd double exposure before him.

To his delight, Djonny saw that the haunted houses appeared shrouded in darkness, even though it was nearing noon. The owners of the tech district surely enjoyed their work bringing such seasonal and timely landscapes to the outer walls of their shops, stores, and service centers.

Djonny had heard rumors that one of the men hired to clean the panels had fallen from his harness. According to the stories, the man had plunged through a white hole into another dimension—one the exact reverse of our own. It was an urban legend usually followed by some sarcastic disbeliever remarking, "How would you know where he landed? Did he contact someone from the other side? Did he call his mother and tell her he was alright, only in reverse?"

This would usually cause the conversation to shift to a story with fewer surreal elements. Perhaps the man had been driven insane from being in two worlds at once. The job, after all, required workers to dangle off the side of the building on ropes and harnesses, swinging in and out of the holograms to wash the panels projecting them. He would have seen the hologram every time he leaned out far enough from the panels to be in or beyond the projection. When he was closer to the wall, he would have seen only the wall. He could have lost his mind trying to keep himself grounded to only one world. The details were there for the eyes, enfolding the worker. For all anyone knew, he might have been driven mad by the details.

Djonny made his way slowly down the street, savoring the story and dreaming up new legends. Some shops displayed the outlines of bats, so finely blended with the rest of the details that they were something a discerning eye had to seek out to find. Other items were more obvious, like the large scarecrow figure on one building, or the giant figure of the Grim Reaper pacing against another. Still another building looked as if it had been there so long that one entire wall had caved in, allowing anyone to walk in through the rubble. Djonny sincerely hoped that no one would try. They would most likely walk through the hologram and smack their head against the building.

Door handles to shops looked like snakes or skulls or demon heads, which only temporarily discouraged anyone from touching them. Doorways gaped like giant open mouths with tongues for doormats. It was all an illusion, a distortion of reality, but it was one he wanted. He could not have planned it better himself.

At the shop where genetically modified pets were sold, bats and winged demons extended from the outer walls, as if growing from it. As their leathery wings reached a certain point, the projected form would burst and dissolve and be drawn back in, giving the illusion of sideways gravity.

Djonny felt compelled to go inside. He had been there many times and knew the owner, a fascinating man named Doctor Virgil

Connor. Virgil was a kind, fatherly type who always wore business attire underneath a white lab coat. He had a crow's nest of hair that was greying just above the ears, and his face was clean-shaven and sincere. The last was an attribute that caused most people to trust him instantly.

Djonny entered the store to its pungent aromas and found Virgil actively engaged with a customer, his bright eyes charged with a background of scientific knowledge.

When Virgil finished with the customer, he walked over to where Djonny was examining the amphibians in their dual-environment cages and tanks. A scurry of salamanders was pressed up against the glass of one tank. As their legs lifted and set again, the air was alive with an osculatory sound, like one thousand miniature lips smacking.

"They sure love the glass," Virgil laughed, turning his attention from Djonny to the tank.

"More than their water?" Djonny asked.

Virgil nodded. "They do spend more time on the glass."

"Perhaps they don't see the difference," Djonny said contemplatively. "Both are clear. One is fluid, the other is a super-fluid. To the salamander's mind, the two might equate."

Virgil looked at Djonny as if he didn't think one so young should have such philosophical thoughts. To his credit, he did not criticize. Instead, he smiled down at Djonny, who was only half his height.

"What are those?" Djonny asked, pointing to the creatures in the adjacent tank.

"Those are Zambian tree frogs. Fascinating little things. See how they rest with one leg dangling off the branch? I think they do that as part of their camouflage. Their legs tend to look like twigs, and their feet like leaves."

"Do you sell a lot of them?"

"Would you like one?" Virgil's tone shifted from friendly scientist to salesman as rapidly as an adrenaline heartbeat.

"No," Djonny said, "I was more interested in your spiders."

"Well, to answer your question, I sell far more frogs than spiders. Although, that may be because people lose the frogs and the frogs escape to where they disappear best: the trees. Then, of course, the customers return to buy another frog."

Djonny smiled at this revelation, then tried to steer the conversation back to his original purpose. "Or it could be that people are afraid of spiders and they think frogs are cute."

"Good observation," Virgil said. "So, shall we wander to the spiders, or would you like to hold one of the amphibians? The salamanders will stick on your arms. Children seem to love that."

Not enjoying the comparison, Djonny spoke as adult-like as he could manage. "I *will* see one of your Zamibian amphibians, though only for a moment."

"Ah," Virgil said, "you know what you want, do you? You're more determined than the average patron, I see." He lifted the lid on the frogs' containment. "And how did you come by this determination? Was it taught, or learned, or both? You see, every creature, even man, has an environment to manipulate unless it manipulates him. Some learn to manipulate more substantially than others. I'm always trying to discover which variety each of my customers represent: manipulator or manipulated."

Having deftly pulled a single branch and frog through the small opening in the top of the tank, Virgil passed it to Djonny.

"When I sell a frog to a customer, I give them the branches for free. The main reason for that is because the frogs love these particular trees. They live where they love, so to speak."

Djonny held the branch. He felt it was an awkward way to look at the frog. The frog's weight pulled the branch in odd directions, threatening to send the frog spinning, though Djonny could see the tree frog was well adapted and would probably continue to cling to the branch even if it was dropped or flipped upside down.

When he decided he'd had enough of the stick, Djonny reached out to grab the frog by hand. The frog made a cute chirping noise and drew its legs up as if readying itself to spring away, but Djonny closed his fingers around it before it could jump. He dropped the branch to the floor, and Virgil picked it up, looking only slightly annoyed.

The frog felt wet and cold in Djonny's grasp. It kept chirping, and he noticed the other frogs in captivity began to mimic the sound. He could feel the frog's tiny hammering heartbeat through its skin, and he tried to console it. "It's okay, little guy. I'm not going to hurt you."

Apparently, the frog did not share the sentiment, because it mobilized its retractable claws and scratched the gripping hand. Four tiny cuts welled up instantly on Djonny's flesh. Each slice stung intensely enough that he cried out and thrust the strange beast away from him.

Virgil scooped the frog up with the stick and placed both back in the glass container. Djonny wanted no more to do with tree frogs and in fact began to wish they would all get lost in the trees. Children could lose those pets, as far as he cared. He surveyed the damage on his hand and found it didn't look as terrible as it felt.

"Do they have claws naturally, or is that a genetic modification?" he asked, but when Virgil replied it sounded as if there was a tin can around the man's mouth.

"At least you didn't get hit by the poisonous one," Virgil said, his words echoing closely.

Djonny assumed the shock of his injury had affected his hearing somehow, especially when Virgil's words echoed again: "At least you got hit by the poisonous one."

Djonny couldn't see Virgil's mouth moving, but he was certain he heard him say again, "At least you didn't get hit by the poisonous one."

To Djonny's dizzy dismay, Virgil pulled him along on a circuit of the entire store, leading him not in the direction of the spiders but from one cage to another, all the while staring directly in his face, extolling the various skills and attributes of every species and variety of animal

Djonny wondered what had come over Virgil to make him act that way. Why was he taking his time getting to the arachnids, and why was he staring at him so much? What was so important about the bifurcated tails of the crocodiles, or the amphibious octopus? How could defanged vampire bats be more important than defanged black widows? Djonny couldn't ask. He had either lost his ability to ask for what he wanted, or he was lost in the kindness of respecting his elders. Whatever the cause, he endured the tour and let Virgil carry on with his encyclopedic knowledge of mammalian and amphibian and arachnoid anatomies.

Before long, Djonny found himself on the street. In his hand was a bulbous, clear container with a black form in the center of it, accompanied by smaller forms that were her food. Though he couldn't remember exiting the store, he already knew the name of the shiny lady in the bubble. She was Enola. Her mysterious nature was as wrapped up in her name as the tiny flies were wrapped up in her webs.

2. See the Seeler Seethe

The tech district came to an end. Djonny came to a storefront he had not seen on any of his previous trips to the downtown area. It was a plain storefront, undecorated by the holograms that adorned the building adjacent to it. Over the door of this plain shop was a wooden sign with the curious designation "Seeler" painted in blue letters. Next to the name, painted in multiple colors, were spools of thread.

A crowd of boys Djonny's age milled around the window in front of the store. Two of the boys nearest him were talking excitedly, making wagers it sounded like. Djonny interrupted them. "What's going on in there?"

One of the boys made a face like the air had suddenly become septic. The other looked at Djonny and said, "The guy in there is sewing up ears and giving out fortunes. We're taking bets on who gets a good fortune and who gets crap."

As he spoke, the crowd erupted in laughter, pointing at the window mockingly.

"Crap!" someone said. "He got crap! Pay up!"

"Noooo! Not again! I won't lose the next one, I swear!" said another.

"Yes, that's two out of three! I'm in the upper bracket! I hope my nose don't bleed!" another boy cried out.

The two boys Djonny had interrupted ignored him and exchanged money. They were too busy counting to continue talking to him, so he interrupted them again.

"How can you tell what they're saying in there?"

"We read lips," said the talkative boy. His friend made an angry face at Djonny again, and both immediately went back to counting.

Djonny watched as two young men entered the shop. They were not much older than him. They were dressed in black, with arabesque designs on their shirts, and one of the boys had the dangling, gaping earlobe-holes of Egyptian fashion. Before they entered, Djonny heard one of the boys say, "This guy is the best. You won't look like a victim anymore. He'll fix you up, any color you want."

Drawn by curiosity, Djonny followed them inside. The store had once been a bakery, but the glass cabinet that lined one of the walls was now filled with the multicolored threads of the new owner's business. The faint smell of baked goods lay just beneath the potent smell of iodine, as if one business had supplanted the other earlier that morning.

The action was being carried out by a less-than-hygienic man in a sweat-stained, armless shirt that was so thin his chest hairs were visible. He wore jeans and dirty leather sandals that let his unpleasant toes out on display for all to see. His nose, a formidable, bulbous growth, was run through with thin, blood-colored threads. In one pudgy hand he held a needle, and in his other was a spool of orange thread.

Before the sweaty workman sat a young man, who was having his earlobes sewn back together after having had them gaged to an enormously ugly circumference. The thread draped neatly from the spool to the needle. The workman passed the needle through ear flesh, drew the thread through until the spool was near the ear, then performed a rapid twisting of his wrists. All five of the witnesses in the room, Djonny included, looked on in amazement as the gaping gage began to close.

Within five minutes, the sweaty man had completed the operation. He handed the young man a hand mirror. He took it, admiring his newly closed earlobes. They were three shades of orange from the mix of thread, iodine, and the slight trickle of blood coming from the wounds. Satisfied, he passed the mirror back.

"My fortune?" the young man asked.

"Oh, yeah, right," the sweaty workman said. "You have two weeks to live. You're going to be hit by a truck going backwards on the freeway."

There was explosive laughter, jeers, and cheers from outside.

The sweaty man handed his patient a tube of ointment. "Apply this every day for the next two weeks. It will keep the wounds open and the bad bacterium at bay." Despite his rough appearance, the man's voice was paternal and jovial. He surveyed the room and asked, "Who's next?"

The next young man in line had an odd, nauseous expression on his face. He took three steps backward and bolted from the store, banging the door closed behind him. The boy with the orange thread in his ears stared sadly at his small tube of ointment and followed slowly out the door.

This left Djonny and the two black-clad young men. The one with the gaged ears was clearly nervous and began asking questions. "How do I know you're going to do a good job? If I don't like it, can I have my money back? How much does it hurt? Do you always give bad fortunes?"

"Hey listen, kid," the sweaty man said, winding up the excess orange thread and dropping the needle into a red plastic bucket, "you don't have to do it today if you're too scared. Why don't you watch while I do a couple more? Then you can see the pain on the faces of the torturees and decide if you even want to come back tomorrow."

"I'm not scared," the boy said defensively. "I just don't know you're qualified to do it, that's all."

"Oh. Well. Look there." The man pointed to a piece of paper that was taped to the wall with black electrical tape. It appeared to be some kind of official document. "That," he claimed, "is my license to seel. Spelled s-e-e-l, after the way of sewing a falcon's eyes shut. I used to be a falconer. A spitting good one, too."

Spittle flew from his lips when he said the word "spitting."

"You should've seen some of my birds," he continued. "Beautiful. As soon as I get enough money, I'm going to buy a new one. I'm getting back into it, and I'm getting my titles back. Good-for-nothing judges. For now, though, I saw that my services were *transferable*, you know what I mean? Sewn ears are in style now. Gaged ears are not. I can sew your ears up quick as I did that last kid. I suppose I could sew your eyes shut too, if you want, like a falcon. You pay me, I don't care what it is. I'll sew it, and you won't feel a thing."

"I think I'll watch you do one more, then I'll decide," the boy stalled. He turned to Djonny and said, "You can go next."

Djonny stared at the sweaty man's veiny nose when he spoke to him. "I want my lips seeled," he told the nose. For a moment, he couldn't believe the words left his mouth, but then the man seemed to confirm Djonny's idea.

"Yeah, well, you don't have no gages, so I can't sew your ears up, can I?"

He showed Djonny to the seat in front of him and retrieved a new half-circle needle from a bag behind him. The needle was in a plastic package, and he ripped it open. "I haven't ever done lips before. But there's a first time for everything, I guess. What color do you want?"

"Black," Djonny said, not sure where the idea came from. His favorite color was green, but for some reason that didn't sound appropriate as a color for the thread that would seel his lips. He looked at the clothing of the black-clad boys and pondered his environment for a moment. Did it have something to do with what

Virgil said earlier? Was Virgil always right?

The man with the drinker's nose held the needle ready. "Sit still," he said. "You don't want me to mess up."

The man applied iodine to the needle with a sponge brush and went expertly through the motions. His hands were very skilled and obviously had much practice in the craft. When he was done, he gave Djonny a tube of ointment with the same advice he had given to the other boy.

"Bacterium at bay and bad open wounds keep for the next two weeks," the man said, his words sounding oddly disjointed. "Apply this every day ointment."

The boy in black, who had told Djonny to go ahead of him, said, "Aren't you going to ask for your fortune?"

His friend nodded in agreement. "Yeah, you can't leave without a fortune."

Djonny just looked at them. His lips were sewn shut. He figured they would understand he couldn't speak, but the boys waited silently, offering no evidence of their attention spans.

The seeler came to their rescue. "His fortune is the best one yet." Turning to Djonny, he said, "When the hologram shows only now, the future is brighter than a field of diodes."

A surprised burst of laughter came from the crowd at the window.

Djonny nodded slowly, his head wobbling as if it had turned to rubber. It sprang back after a moment, and he was glad for that. His head, heavy on the neck of flesh, felt tough yet springy—giving him the impression his head had been replaced with that of a frog. Was it the head of a frog or the whole frog that had taken the space where his head used to be? He had no way of knowing; there were no mirrors anywhere nearby.

The sweaty seeler raised the hand mirror to Djonny's face. In the distorted glass, his lips looked twice the size they should have been. He was staring into a handheld funhouse, not a portable vanity. Despite the distended lips, the rest of his head still looked human, and so he had that to comfort him.

He paid the sweaty man and left, looking straight ahead, avoiding the stares from the crowd of boys exchanging money outside.

3. How to Play Baseball on the Subway

One city block away from the former bakery, Djonny looked into the street and saw three frogs leaping down a storm drain. Before it followed his two frog brothers down, Djonny thought he saw the third frog gesture with a webbed digit, eyes pointed to the sky.

Djonny looked up to see a banner flying in the sky. Following it down, he saw that the banner was attached to a pole, and the pole was attached to a building. The building lay outside of the tech district and was not adorned with a hologram façade. It had seen many years on the same avenue. Its paint was thick and impenetrable. The walls were thick too, perhaps thicker for every coat of paint that had been applied over the years. A large sign framed with flashing lights sat atop the building, and a single word was etched into the sign and traced with glow-in-the-dark paint: Bowman. The lights flashed on and off in patterns that danced and caught the attention of all passersby.

Djonny stepped up to the storefront and looked at a poster taped to the inside of the display window. The poster described a game of potential death in which players could hunt one another, brother against brother, mother against son. Upon the poster was the picture of a musclebound man standing in a ring of fire with three arrows jutting from his back. He was in the act of beheading two opponents at once with a heavy metal scimitar. The line at the bottom of the poster claimed participants would have the "pleasure" of being televised, having all of their loved ones die, and becoming filthy rich. The sport was called The Running Game. The words *Sign up inside!* were emblazoned across the poster.

Djonny scrunched his nose in distaste and turned away, threading his way through the tricky pedestrian traffic and heading home.

Instead of walking all the way, he turned and dropped down the twelve and a half steps to the subway, hoping there was a train available soon. His feet were tired, sweaty, and throbbing inside his boots and were beginning to feel as if they had lost circulation from walking on the hard cement walkways of the city.

Djonny slid his card through the slot and swung the turnstile, stepping over the intersection of rails where subway trains ran in different directions. Soon enough, he found a train that would take him where he wanted to be and got on board.

He took a seat that was next to no one, propped his feet up on the armrest of the seat beside him, and right away felt better for the change in position. Three young men with clownish black-and-white face paint got on, followed by four punks dressed in baseball uniforms.

The punks immediately took seats near the door, while the clowns approached Djonny. They surrounded him and drove their faces close to his in an obvious ploy to intimidate him. Djonny only rolled his eyes upward and cradled his crystal ball tighter so the clowns wouldn't try to snatch it away. He wanted to make it all the way home with his new pet.

One of the clowns wore face paint drawn in the shape of lightning bolts, one crossing each of his eyes vertically. The rest of his face was a field of white. He put his face so close to Djonny's that Djonny could smell what the boy had eaten for lunch: something with lots of mayonnaise. The clown spoke to his friends without pulling his face away. "There's something terribly wrong with this one."

"What's wrong with him, Rob?" one of the clowns asked. "Is he a variant, or a vagrant?" He had smeared black paint around his lips, with similar smears around each eye. Beside him stood the last of the three, his black lips drooping downward in the saddest of clown frowns.

The frowning clown spoke up timidly, as if feeling pressured to say something. "He's not either, is he? I bet he's a vandal."

The smeared-paint clown thrust an elbow at the frowning clown. "Shut up!" he barked.

The frowning clown shoved back. In an instant, they were face to face, ready to fight.

While this was going on, Rob, the lightning bolt clown, was studying Djonny's threaded lips. "He's no vandal, either," he announced. "Not a vagrant, not a villain, or a vulture. I think he's a vaudevillian."

The two rasslers paused their fake fight long enough to ask, "Like us?"

"No," Rob said, "not like us. He's voiceless. A mime."

"A mime!" said frown clown, and coming from him, the word sounded absolutely degrading. "Let's throw him off the train."

Rob, who had not moved from the severe vicinity of Djonny's face, began to agree when he was struck in the side of the mouth by a baseball.

The three clowns spun around to look in the direction the baseball had come. Four punks in baseball uniforms sat at the opposite end of the train car, pretending there was something extremely interesting about their shoes—and that baseballs might appear out of nowhere and smack people upside the head, only because nature willed it. No other reasoning was needed; shoes were admired.

The tension on the train car stretched, and time followed suit. Djonny thought the clowns might rush the baseball punks, but he also thought the baseball punks looked much more fit than the clowns. Numbers were certainly on the side of the baseball punks as Djonny silently counted himself among them. If a fight broke out between the two equally odd gangs, Djonny would fight for the baseballers. After all, they hadn't threatened to throw Djonny from the train or gotten up tight in his face. They had protected him, and he would return the favor if needed.

One of the baseball punks stood up slowly and deliberately, flexing his sturdy arms. He hefted a short club shaped like a baseball bat. It was a direct taunt, a show of power. The clowns stood their ground, unmoving. None of them appeared to have a weapon.

Would they take the challenge? Djonny thought they would run the other way instead, considering the scared looks on their faces. The subway was slowing, so maybe they would escape when it landed at the boarding station.

The clown with the smeared paint rushed first. He was quicker than he looked, and he managed to dodge the swinging club. As he did, he leapt toward an unarmed member of the baseball team, feigning a punch and throwing an elbow into the ribs of his prey. The elbow struck, and the punk shouted in pain. This sound was encouraging to the other clowns, and they followed their crazed friend into the frenzy.

In a matter of seconds, many things happened. Two more elbows were thrown, some with punks attached, others with clowns.

Rob, whose name Djonny thought might be indication of his pastime activities and whose fists were flying everywhere, got his face smashed in the thin cushions of the seats on the train.

The club transferred hands twice. It found purchase only once.

The seat, which had accepted the clown's face, now held its imprint.

At no time did Djonny see that his services were necessary to aid the baseball punks.

Soon, they were all pushing away from each other. The frowning clown muttered curses under his breath. He had received the unfriendliest of blows: a knee to his soft parts. It had been a matter of friendly fire.

"If I ever see you on this train again . . ." the smeared-faced clown threatened.

A motion from behind the clowns interrupted the cycle of violence that would have repeated, and two old men in suits stepped into the train car. One had bird-like facial features. The other had a sallow toad expression permanently affixed to his face.

The men approached Djonny and sat down next to him, eyeing him hungrily. The old man with the toad-like face bent over and retrieved the baseball from the floor. He stuffed it in his coat pocket, looking around to see if anyone would challenge him on his new acquisition. When no one did, he turned his quiet attention back to Djonny.

The clowns and the baseball punks all found seats and made themselves suddenly silent and civil, looking at Djonny with sincere pity. Djonny got the tingling sensation that a potential beating would have been preferable to being seated beside the two suited men and their authoritative animal auras.

4. The Execution of the Ambient

Traveling through the dingy, grey city with his new threads and a handful of crystal ball, Djonny was accompanied by the strange men to the private road that led to his home. They smelled familiar but looked like no one he had ever met before. How they had come to be his escorts was something of a mystery to him.

One of the men, the one with a face like a toad, bulging eyes, and extremely wide downturned mouth, spoke to him. "We'll need to speak with your parents. Send them out."

Djonny listened closely to the man's words, hoping for clues to where they had come from. None came. The demand to speak with his parents was all that was said. The other man, a bird-like gentleman in a thin suit, simply nodded repeatedly as if agreeing with everything spoken and unspoken.

They walked the reconstituted concrete path to Djonny's house. Sculpted hedges leered at them with the faces of badgers, hyenas, and vultures. For Djonny, these faces were like landmarks. If for some reason they ceased to be there, he would think he was at the wrong house.

Djonny's dad had a love of beautiful gardens, and since the family had the finances, they had a complete grounds crew to work on the yard. The house itself was a sprawling monstrosity with gables sharp and imposing, many high windows, and a stone foundation that tapered out and away, as if built for a massive flood or possibly to prevent a peasant invasion—although peasants had not inhabited the area for four hundred years. The house was like a fortress on the outside. Inside, it was comfortable and clean.

Djonny entered at the side of his house but did not invite his followers in. Even if he tried, his words would have come out as a mumble. Would they even understand? He let the door slam behind him, crossed through the mudroom, and went in the kitchen. In the kitchen, he kicked off his leather boots and made them land back in the mudroom. Bounding up the stairs to his room, he met no one. The house was quiet, as if uninhabited.

His room was the same as he had left it. A collision of books had happened on the bookshelf, and indeed was still happening. There, Carroll's looking glass met with Dahl's chocolate factory, and Lumley's vampires crashed against Barker's thieves. The bed was covered, though not neatly, as if it had been done up by a clumsy teenager. In the corner was his desk and general workspace. There, he had the strata of starts of many an invention—his own personal tech district, where his music sometimes met binary computations. Devices of gadgetry had been dissected there, and some of their remains were evident.

His head ached, but he didn't know why. Was it the idea of inventing something? Was it the newly stitched portion of his countenance? Was it from the strange events at the modified pet store, or from the fight on the train? Was it the feeling of responsibility for his new pet? Or was it possibly a combination of all these things?

Regardless of the answer, if anyone asked, he could give none; his new facial threads limited his speech to unintelligible grunts. Djonny sat on his bed and picked up a remote control from his nightstand. He keyed in a series of numbers and was rewarded with the peaceful sound of music coming from the area of his desk.

The playlist was comprised of sounds he'd captured months ago on the uptown subway. The recording played back the sounds of subway passengers talking, to which Djonny had added a smooth electronic beat. The result was like listening to music with headphones on while simultaneously carrying on a conversation. His favorite part was coming up, and he waited for it with anticipation.

A woman was talking. "Of all the things he could take," she said, "why my Venus flytrap?" The beat slowed when she said "Venus flytrap," and her voice grew distorted, pitch-shifted to match the beat. Her devotion to her flytrap lent the recording an eerie atmosphere.

Djonny's own devotion pooled up inside his head. He suddenly felt the shame of knowing he had already neglected his new pet. Where was she? He mentally retraced his steps.

The spider went in the fish tank?

He recalled Virgil telling him, "This sort of cage is extremely temporary. It's made of sugar. You can see through it now, but if it begins to get cloudy, you've let it sit too long. Don't let your pet remain in the sugar globe so long the globe gets cloudy. Put some water on it with the pet in its new cage. Wherever the water touches, the globe will dissolve, and your black widow will crawl out to its new home. Or put some flies in there and they'll eat through it, then the spider will eat the flies."

Now Djonny remembered. Only moments ago, he had left the globe floating on top of the water of his fish tank. He hoped he wasn't losing his memory. He shook his head to clear his mind and focused on the tank.

His one and only fish was a Betta. Her name was Penumbra. Her body was mostly orange, with a dark, wavy stripe down her center. Djonny looked closely but only saw the taint of the sugar globe on the surface of the fish tank water. There was no sign of the black widow he had purchased from Virgil's Modified Pet Store.

He worried she had been eaten by the Betta. Females could sometimes be incompatible when forced to live together.

They need their own space to behave as females do, Djonny realized. *Penumbra is no exception.*

She had probably grown hungry, seen the spider skating on the water, and deduced that she was food. Djonny had seen Penumbra feed on live things before. It would have been quick. The spider would have gone down in one swift gulp. He hoped it was a mercifully painless death.

As he watched, he saw the fish shudder. It was such a rapid motion that Djonny thought he might have imagined it. No fish ever shuddered like that.

The motion repeated. The fish was convulsing. Djonny supposed she could have seizures like any other animal, but he worried that he might lose two pets in one day.

Penumbra looked like she was going to start floating upside down at any moment. Her eyes were bulging, and her color had drained out. She was certainly sick. Her medium was underwater. She had no way of communicating with him. She began driving herself against the glass sides of the tank. Her convulsions were growing in such ferocity that a crack was forming in the tank. Could she have the strength to break her own tank? Could Penumbra so forcefully shudder as to shatter her home?

Djonny stood by, ready to find out, thinking of ways to save the fish should her strength be adequate to crack the glass.

The strength was there, and the crack became large enough that water began to drip from it. Penumbra smacked against the glass like a demented fish determined to do damage to herself or her confinement. The water leaked out onto the floor. Djonny, her only possible savior, ran for a container.

He returned with a large plastic cup filled with water, but he was too late. Penumbra was lying on her side in the shallow water that remained at the bottom of her tank.

She brought about her own execution, Djonny thought.

He stood and watched the black stripe down her center become a dusty grey swath. He was about to reach in and pick her up to deposit her in the plastic cup, but stopped when he saw her mouth making its last gasping motions.

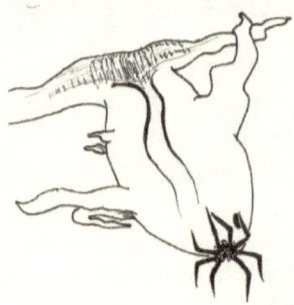

Penumbra stopped moving her mouth, and something stirred within her. Djonny angled his head for a better look. Reaching from inside Penumbra's mouth were multiple pawing black picks. The picks pressed and stretched her mouth until it opened wide enough to allow Enola to escape. She squeezed her thick abdomen through Penumbra's mouth and emerged triumphantly. Then she turned and began to spread some of the blue and white fish tank rocks back onto Penumbra, as if to bury her.

Perhaps this was instinct, Djonny thought, but the action felt as if it had a sense of emotion.

Djonny was amazed but confused. He realized Enola had poisoned Penumbra from inside. In the competition, inevitable among these two females, Enola had vanquished her would-be devourer.

The truth he had come upon earlier about two females not being able to share space seemed prophetic at this new turn of events. He couldn't make such accurate assessments every day. He swore that next time he had a thought like that, he was going to write it down and preserve it for future generations.

Djonny supposed the only thing he could do now was wait for an appropriate time to remove the fish to a more respectful resting place. Under the rocks of her fish tank seemed so disrespectful that Djonny had his own shudder at the prospect of such a cold death and burial.

He watched in awe as Enola crept to a shady corner of the tank behind one of the ornaments, a fake plant made of plastic. There she rested and watched. The fish convulsed no more, but the spider still possessed the instinct to be wary.

26

Djonny made plans to find Enola some flies and find Penumbra a true burial place. He cast a glance toward his workspace. It was ready for him, and now he was ready for it. His responsibility to his pets would wait. Spiders, he had learned, could go for months without food. He, on the other hand, could not. It was time for him to do some inventing.

While he considered using straws to help him drink, the music worked on him. He soon realized that the great thing about being alone like Enola was that the individual could be perfected. He would create new items for his new condition, figure ways to get crackers and cheese in his mouth without making a mess all over his face, and discover himself in the process—or so he decided to try.

The music prodded him in directions he had not considered since watching the battle of the modified pets. He thought about methods of communication. How was he going to talk to people if his lips were seeled? How was he going to explain why he did it? Would he have to walk around with a sign on his back with answers to the most frequently asked questions? Would he need to learn sign language?

Guiding him, the music said, "Take me, drink me, use me . . ."

That was it! He would take the music with him. He would find a way to let the music speak for him. After all, who better to speak for one who is no longer able than the perfect pitch, voice, and harmony of the greatest musicians? Emotion was the motivation behind speech. Djonny decided that from now on, he would communicate using the medium most capable of invoking emotion: music.

5. Aphrodisiac Jacket

Djonny slid on the jacket and felt Zen with it. He was once again whole. Now he had second skin and second speech. How he might invent second sight was beyond his present learning. The jacket was a thin black leather. Speakers had been fitted inside of it, with vents to let out the sound. A three-terabyte media utility device was connected to the speakers, and Djonny practiced scrolling rapidly through the selections with the first three digits of his right hand. He had the option of finding sound bites by artist names, album titles, or even by the very words he wished to communicate. Lyrics were available and accessible. If in a pinch, not remembering any specific bite with his desired choice of words, he could simply type in the words he wanted to say and watch all the possibilities be brought up for him.

He tested it in front of his mirror.

"Hello, hello, hi. I'm Djonny. I'm the deejay. And who are you? Who do you think you are? You know what you are? You're a . . ."

Djonny was pleased with himself. He had even included a way to record sounds.

There were a thousand songs with his own name in it: "Jonny, Jonny, Jonny. Be good . . . Jonny."

He imagined he would never have to speak again. There would always be music. And it seemed the music kept coming. The industry had transformed over the years, that was certain, but the magnitude—the volume—of musical selections available was so gargantuan that it looked almost infinite.

Infinite music.

Djonny turned to look at his own big supply and noticed the clock. The time was all wrong! How could it be that time already? He was late for school! He had to get there fast. He couldn't possibly skip it if he didn't go first.

He wound a circuitous path through his house to get himself out the door to school. Pants, shirt, socks—all were thrown on in haste. In his rush down the hall, he saw a door near the stairs where no door had been before. Pausing only momentarily to look at it, he saw that the door was white and wide and had a bright blue light shining from beneath it.

From within somewhere, he heard a sound like the cadence of voices. He doubted his parents would be there at such an hour. They had their own schedules during the day. But if it wasn't them, then who?

With too many unknown elements, he decided he did not want to go through the door or see anything come out of it. So he scooted cautiously around it.

At school, it was the usual sport of swimming through rivers of human flesh that constituted the hallways. As soon as he arrived, he got an alphanumeric message from one of his friends, Darrel Cox. Djonny found his way through the thousands as he read the message.

Nice 2 C U, D J walker read the message, both simple and complex.

Djonny answered: *Are you already in class, Darrel Licked?*

Darrel was quick with the comeback: *Of course, Main E Yak.*

You the eyes and ears and mouth? Djonny typed. He thought a moment and sent the next thumb mail: *Double Dog Darrel.*

Hey! Don't call me that. I don't associate with them.

Oh, sorry! Djonny replied, sincerely, remembering the group of girls at school who were classified as the Double Dog Dares. He added: *I've never met them.*

Well, Darrel responded, *hope you never do, Jaw Knee.*

Djonny didn't reply to the last jab because he was walking past the low wall where the mature girls always sat. One of them, he noticed, was only wearing socks; no shoes. The strange style distracted him momentarily, but then he came to the place where he and his friends most often congregated: in the lobby of the theater wing, in a wide, cool space where a few other cliques also gathered.

Among those he recognized, there were also some he did not. Talking to his friend, Sam-O, was a princess of Nihil. She of dark clothing and probably even darker thoughts was unknown to Djonny, though he knew her kind. Head-to-toe black clothing, dyed black hair, and pale face. One of Djonny's friends, Pam Ravi, probably knew this new girl. In fact, they probably shared cosmetic secrets.

Also, there was Kevin and Beto, a couple of Djonny's best friends. Beside them was another face previously unknown to him: a tall boy with tall teeth and not enough lips to cover them, with a t-shirt of a surfing werewolf.

"Friends," came the melodic voice from the speakers in Djonny's jacket, "who are these new people?"

Beto came forward and noticed Djonny's change without answering the question. "Your face is wounded, no? What did you do, bite an alligator?" Beto's humor was evident by the wide grin on his face.

Not expecting this kind of response, Djonny was lost for an answer. He diverted and chose a song he knew Beto liked: "A Huevo" by Los Straitjackets and the Trashmen. It was an effective change of subject.

"Good one," Beto said, swinging his hips as if he were dancing with a woman.

Pleased by the act of pleasing another, Djonny let the music continue. There weren't many words in the song anyway, and he couldn't use them as his own words. Instead, he relaxed and let the mood roll down the hall. A few girls came by and saw Beto dancing with himself. They giggled, but it was a friendly sound, not mocking. A crowd began to gather, and Djonny was proud to hear people telling him they were impressed. His invention was a hit, so far.

One bold young man made a request. "Hey, man, you got 'Dracula from Houston'?"

It made sense to Djonny that this should be an immediate request. Hearing one surf song made people's minds associate other songs with surfing ties. Djonny nodded and let "A Huevo" blend into "Dracula."

"Hey, that was incredible," said one girl in the crowd. Her wavy blonde hair made her stand out among the others, especially the standard goth issues. Djonny didn't know her, although he had seen her around. Christy something. "Do you do parties?" she asked.

Taking only a second and a half to think about it, Djonny responded musically, pausing the melody only briefly to inject: "I am . . . in parties. I am . . . the deejay. I'm *your* deejay."

She smiled with her eyes, making Djonny step back a little, unsure of how to interpret it. Girls had never smiled at him much before, and they especially never smiled at him with their eyes.

Before he could consider this new feeling much further or start a new song, the final first bell rang. Conditioned response drove them all toward the doors; the crowd became glazed of eyes and shuffling of feet.

Beto was less hypnotized than the rest, though he was still on the move. He turned to Djonny and said, "I can't handle my Mariposa class today, so I'm going to hang outside the ladies' and say 'Hey' to all the ladies as they come and go. See you in gym, *mijo*?"

Djonny nodded. *"Por supuesto, mijo."*

Trudging the same direction as everyone else, Djonny remembered the message from his friend Darrel and decided to answer as he departed. He let the thumb pads type *See you later, Weir Dough*. Then he smiled and waved at a security camera as he passed under it.

As the hallways cleared, a voice filled the emptying spaces through the power of the intercom: "If you can hear this message, you're on your way to graduation. One day closer to freedom and a ten-dollar bill in your pocket. Lunch money, some might say, but we say, 'Get a haircut, you bum.' Oh, and if you can't hear this message, we'll say it louder next time. For those of you in outer space already this morning, oh well, just like, never mind."

Homeroom was where Djonny was supposed to be, so he mimicked the others and shuffled his feet in the direction of his class. As he approached the classroom door, he noticed a gaggle of girls there, whispering and giggling. The closer Djonny got, the louder the giggling became. When he was within a couple of feet from them, one of their number began laughing hysterically and pointing at Djonny's face. Another of them held up a hand, palm toward the hyena, obviously condoning the laughter, and as she dismissed, so she stepped toward Djonny and planted her lips on his.

Djonny stopped in his tracks, wondering if he had won a bet. The girl who had kissed him strutted back to her friends with her palm out expectantly. The palm was soon favored with money from all sides, and Djonny realized she was the one who had won the bet.

Unable to think of anything to play that might fit the situation, but realizing he was supposed to be caring for his new threads, Djonny ignored musical comebacks and retrieved the ointment from his pocket to spread some on his seeled lips.

To this sight, the girls let out a mutual "Ewww!"

Behind him and out of his sight, a boy with metal braces on his teeth was busy spreading wax on the braces to keep them from cutting his lips.

Djonny opened the door to the classroom. Following him as he entered were the words, "I can't believe you did that, Kay! Completely gross." The door closed, and he heard no more from the Double Dog Dares.

Finding his assigned seat, Djonny saw that there was a large, fresh wad of chewing gum deposited on it. He did not sit but put the toe of his boot next to the wad and catapulted it across the room. It flew past the teacher's aide and smacked wetly against a bulletin board with paper cutout letters that read *If you bring gum, you must bring enough for everyone.* The wad of gum stuck there for a moment until its weight brought it to the floor with a splat.

His seat was still sticky with gum residue and slobber, so he turned, pushed the desk section of his seat loudly against the wall, and perched there rather than sitting. His teacher gave him a look of hardness. Djonny responded with a shrug.

In the hall, there were loud voices and arguing. All eyes in the class turned to the door as it opened. All eyes grew afraid when they saw who was there.

It was the meanest psycho in the whole school, Mick Jocctyn, also known as Sick Mick. Even the administration feared him.

Mister Eft, the teacher, was no exception. As Mick entered the classroom, Mister Eft rolled his chair back toward the glass wall by the hall.

There was something about Mick, aside from his square jaw and squinty eyes, that made people work hard at appeasing his every whim. Mick was one of those who inspired fear because of his unpredictability. Like any psychotic personality, he would act out unnaturally, and these episodes of tantrum and tempest were what fed people's fear.

Mick looked into Djonny's eyes, easily spotting him since he was seated higher than all the rest. Djonny tried to look into Mick's eyes but saw only pinched flesh where the eyes should have been. The squint was impenetrable.

Reaching in his jacket, Mick stepped briskly toward Djonny. "You kissed my girl?" he screamed. "You're dead!"

A few who had not previously seen Mick in action gasped as his hand come out of his jacket. They may have thought he would produce a gun or some other weapon, but instead he brought out a white paint pen. Those who gasped now sighed, though their breathiness was not over. One among them even managed to say "Oo, Mick's gonna hurt that little boy Djonny" as Mick tagged Djonny's jacket. The gaspers drew their breath in and held it. When Mick was done with his sign, they let out their sighs.

Djonny said simply, "It ain't easy to kiss . . ."

Mick told him, "I tagged you. We fight after school," and then walked out the classroom door, unchallenged.

6. How Did Anyone Get Angry Before Heavy Metal?

The paint pen had a chemical smell to it, and it was bothering him, so Djonny went to a window and let it open a crack-and-a-half. Mister Eft made to protest, but Djonny prevented him from saying anything with, "We all need fresh air, and birds and trees . . ."

With that sound bite playing, Djonny perched himself again on top of his desk. The other teenage children in the class (Homeroom, they called it, though it wasn't feeling at all homey) all stared at him. Some looks were contemptuous; others were pitying. Djonny wanted neither.

He tried to take his mind off the cold stares and considered ways he could have battled the girl, Kay, to keep her from kissing him: shoving her away, ducking and dodging, zipping his face up in his jacket. Each of his imaginary situations ended with the girl offended. Sick Mick tagged the jacket at the end of every scenario. Djonny couldn't find a way out of it, though his mind kept trying.

"You stink!" one of the girls in Homeroom said loudly, startling him from his daydreams. She was looking directly at him and refused to turn her eyes away at his glance. She kept talking. "How does Djonny stink? Everyone wants to know."

Emboldened by the girl, a boy named Sean spoke up as well. "He stinks like . . . like . . . stinky cheese." His eyes met Djonny's, and they did a brief battle for the space between. Djonny was winning.

Another boy, Xavier, spoke, and Djonny lost the eye battle with Sean. Xavier said, "He stinks like my gym locker." Then the eyes again.

Soon, ten more pairs of eyes were staring at Djonny, growing red in their dislike, the dislike slipping toward hatred.

More eyes came down the hall outside the classroom. These eyes belonged to adults. Adults in audit mode. The adult eyes stared, and adult fingers pointed toward the teens in their confinement. This keen group of professionals, dressed in business casuals and carrying tablets and taking notes, passed slowly, as if perusing the unfathomable yet contained wild that was a full set of teenagers in a classroom setting.

They scrutinized the class but kept walking, and were almost gone from view when Mister Eft realized they were there. He jumped from his seat to press his hands and face against the glass. He moaned, "Take me with you," as his hands made embarrassing kissing noises against the smooth surface. The group of self-assured adults remained for a short moment to regard this embarrassing action that clearly separated Mister Eft from their social status.

He was on the wrong side of the glass.

The adults ceased pointing and staring and continued their tour, leaving Mister Eft to watch them go. He let himself off the window and slumped his shoulders as he turned back to his desk and chair. He clearly detested his station, but when he caught the taint of chemical on the air, his face curled up in the center around his nose in a manner that showed he had another thing to hate. He and all the students in the class had a target for their aggression.

The between-class bell rang. Everyone, including Mister Eft, headed for the door. They all wanted away from Djonny and his paint-scented jacket.

As Djonny was leaving with the rest of them, he accidentally bumped shoulders against a girl whose face, temples, and chin were decorated with acne.

"Excuse me," he said timidly.

The girl curled her lip up in a snarl and told him, "There's no excuse for you."

A boy pushed Djonny back, ushering the girl ahead through the door.

Djonny waited, even stepped backward as people jostled out the door. Once the room was finally empty, he took himself out to the currents of backpacks and blue jeans, pimples and prepubescent body odor.

In the hallway, hall urchins began to notice the symbol on his jacket. They began to avoid him—and as more avoided him, so did they all. It was herd mentality at its most direct. Djonny had Mick's sign on him. Mick now owned him.

Djonny knew fear would follow him for the rest of the day. He could see it in the eyes of those who got too close before noticing the sign on him. When they saw it, they would spin and turn and lurch away, pushing against others to get out of his way and to show they wanted nothing to do with him.

In spite of the fear that followed him, Djonny found comfort in the fear bubble that encircled him. It was almost as if the graffito symbol on his jacket gave him power, buffeting the inferiors around him, giving him more freedom than he'd ever had. At least that was one way to look at it, so he did.

Never one to wallow in the mud of negativity, Djonny found an appropriate sound bite, and though it was sad, delivered it with a smile: "Where one might find solace in a shotgun sandwich . . ."

Sam-O approached with a friendly smile but dropped it when he saw Djonny's new unfriendly decoration. Holding his hands up as if to push Djonny away, Sam-O said, "Hey, looks like you found some trouble today, huh?"

"Everywhere I look, I see it," Djonny's sing-song voice replied.

Keeping his distance, Sam-O asked, "Is that Mick's sign?"

"Yeah, the schizo, psycho, weirdo, wrote . . . on my jacket."

"Did he challenge you to a fight?"

"He didn't invite me to a party, if you know what I mean."

Sam-O nodded with a serious frown. "Maybe you should run away. The last kid Mick fought is in Northeast."

"That right?"

"Oh yeah." Sam-O nodded, encouraged by the details. Unable to stop now, he elaborated: "The last kid went psycho himself, and no one dared pin the fight on Mick, so the *other* kid got sent to the 'bad-kid' school. The fight started out normal, punching and kicking, that sort of thing. Then Mick got real freaky and started choking the kid. One of the hall monitors stopped the fight, or the kid might've died."

"A hall monitor . . . actually saw it?"

"Right, but it was one of Mick's buddies, so of course he didn't tell anyone anything. I don't think he's a hall monitor anymore. Somebody was smart enough and brave enough to kick him out. He still terrorizes everybody as much as Mick. I don't know his name. He was in Gardner's class with us, remember?"

"Third grade? Not many memories . . ."

"It doesn't matter anyway, I guess. You need to worry about Mick more than his spies."

"Spies?"

"Oh yeah," Sam-O agreed, then realized what he was trying to warn Djonny about. He took several furtive glances around at the teeming teens. "I've probably spent too much time with you already. See you later, if you haven't decided to run away. Oh, and don't call on me to be your backup. I'm fragile." And with that admission, he disappeared into the crowd.

"Friend, foe, no one knows . . . Friend apocalypse," Djonny responded to no one in particular.

The only question on his mind now was whether he would be a casualty or a survivor.

7. If You Can't Sing, SCREAM!!

The intercom called out: "Principal Byrd would like to remind you all that the test comes before the testimony. SATs are next week, ACTs are the following week, and DCTs are the week after that. Prepare to be tested beyond your wildest dreams."

Algebra was taught by a man who never removed his sunglasses. Though no one had definitive proof he was blind, it was the general gossip that he was—and some of his actions tended to confirm the rumors.

He could hear the most subtle of sounds. By mysterious means, he could identify a student within his class without even turning his attention from the chalkboard.

"Glen," he might say, "why are you passing notes to Candace?" And he would do this without seeing either of them.

The greater mystery came when he would write or read something—for how could he do those things unless he had the power of sight?

"Give me the note," he might say to Candace, and she would of course comply. He might begin reading, and Glen would be astonished that the reading was word for word: "Candace, do you like Foamy Malt?"

Through inevitable laughs, giggles, and snickers, the teacher's head would rise from the paper, the sunglasses always obscuring his eyes so that no one could really know if he saw them or not, but he would say to Glen, "And is this the time to be conducting relationship polls? During my math lesson?"

Glen would have no choice but to agree that it was the wrong time, saying something obsequious such as, "No, Mister Morgen, it's not the time."

Mister Morgen would then toss the note and resume his lesson.

While this imagined scenario between Glen and Candace and Mister Morgen ran through Djonny's mind, someone slipped him a note. He glanced up from his imaginings to see who had passed him the paper. He only caught sight of the red hair as the messenger loped out the door without being detected by the teacher. It was interesting how someone could show such a high level of professionalism at such a young age. This messenger was like the ones who would go far in life. They were the ones who went toward their desires as if nothing was in their way.

Djonny realized he had a note in his hand. Examining it, he saw it was half of a full sheet, folded twice. Inside was scratchy writing that spelled out: *I'm going to CRUSH you with my bare hands! — Mick*

Threats from Mick by messenger. Now *that* was an interesting twist. If Djonny wasn't so worried about the psycho doing something really unexpected, he might have laughed a lot more about the whole situation. He might have started making jokes about the surprise of knowing Mick could read and write, so what next? Would he find out Mick had other talents no one knew about, like macramé? Would he find out Mister Morgen could see everything just fine and had no need for the pretense of blindness? One was a mystery worth solving. The other, a mystery of the psychotic-episode kind.

In all of Djonny's time in Mister Morgen's classes, he had never witnessed even a tilting of the glasses. No sign had he ever seen of the man's supposed blindness, nor had he ever seen any obvious sign of Mister Morgen's sight. The mystery remained mysterious. Never had Djonny seen a white cane, and never had he seen a dilating or contracting pupil.

As Djonny explored the possibilities, he noticed the formulae Mister Morgen was writing on his beloved chalkboard. The chalk made a pleasant, scratchy squeak as Morgen wrote:

24/7=____

And he wrote: *53xY=17 Y=____*

And he wrote: *exp1Ode*

As Mister Morgen wrote the last line, there came a violent shriek from somewhere outside the classroom, and the chalk slid at an angle horribly wrong, causing it to make a noise that brought pain to every single one of the six hundred and thirty-nine teeth in the room.

Mister Morgen swayed dizzily. He dropped the chalk into the tray at the base of the chalkboard. He turned and raised his hands up near his head. For a brief moment, Djonny thought the man might actually pull the sunglasses off of his face, but that wasn't what he did. Instead, he cupped his palms against his head and shook it like a swimmer with water in his ears. He then turned back to the chalkboard, erased the last alphanumeric rambling, and wrote a new one, which had an obvious direction of inspiration:

24/a7x=scream

To which one student, whose name was pronounced "He-Row,"

raised a hand. The student next to Hiro, whose name was Craig and pronounced it "Kreg," obviously did not want the attention Hiro was bringing to that side of the room, and so crouched his head down, slouched his butt forward, and avoided all possible eye contact.

Mister Morgen, who had not turned and couldn't necessarily make eye contact with anyone but appeared to be admiring his own writing skills on the board, said, "Yes, Hiro, you have a question?"

"Is it okay to have an A on both sides of the equation?" Hiro asked.

"No, never."

"But—" Hiro began.

Mister Morgen cut him off. "An equation sometimes requires simplification. Your job is to simplify and create true equality. By the way, once you've finished with that one, I would like you to graph the 'scream.' Can you do that?"

Hiro nodded, as did seven other pupils in the class. The rest stared numbly on.

Mister Morgen said, "Very good, get to work." He turned to face the class and took his seat.

Despite having his head down, Craig noticed the turning of the teacher and managed to make himself even less visible by slouching more, so that his spine was curved like a letter J turned sideways.

Djonny had the work done in his head already, but he busied himself with the paperwork, if only because it was expected of him. While he did that, he pondered the possibility of Mister Morgen's glasses having mirrors on them. It would explain how he knew when things were going on behind him. A simple trick of reflected light, that's all it was. Djonny was only slightly convinced of this. But what of the other tricks?

Looking up from his desk, Mister Morgen seemed to focus on Djonny—but how could anyone know for sure? "Is anyone finished with the first problem?" he asked.

Leaving his hands on the desk, Djonny raised the index finger of his left hand.

"Djonny?"

It was not only expected, but almost foreshadowed. Djonny somehow knew he would be called upon. He sighed behind his threads and moved his hands to talk, saying, "Yes . . . I've done all you've asked, and more . . ."

"Have you finished all the problems, then?"

Djonny waxed impudent with, "Not then . . . but now . . ."

"Hmm," Morgen noted, "your voice sounds different, but the overconfidence is the same. Why don't you grace us with your answer to the first problem?"

"Don't you want to give it . . . to one of the lesser . . .?"

Morgen shook his head, though it was not meant as denial since he called on Harold, a large, cumbersome child in the back of the class. "Harold. Do you have an answer for the first equation I wrote on the board?"

Harold sat behind Craig, and Craig exerted such skill in his stillness that the very air around him became more than air. It became aura. Still, silent aura.

"Nah," said Harold, "but it's too easy. It's how many hours in a week."

"Ah, good observation," Morgen said, "but that would be written this way, wouldn't it?" Morgen stood, spun, and wrote quickly: *24x7=____*

Harold puzzled over the equation long enough that Morgen turned his attention back to Djonny. It could not have passed his attention that at least four of his students returned to their answers to change things.

"Djonny? Would you like to answer now?"

"It's too easy," Djonny said, repeating Harold's words, stalling because he was struggling trying to think of songs that had numbers for lyrics. He succeeded, however slowly. "Three . . . point four . . . and about three . . ."

"Why answer so slowly? Not your usual—"

"Converted to hours . . . it would be . . . three hours and . . . twenty-six minutes."

Mister Morgen did his standing spin turn and wrote the conversion on the board, the chalk moving rapidly, his fingers doing quick work of the proof. "It appears to be correct. Now, do you have an answer for Y?"

"Because my lips are seeled. I speak with music . . ."

Mister Morgen thought about that for a second. "Clever, but I meant the variable of Y."

"Oh, sure . . . three and a . . . repeating remainder . . . sixteen places."

Again, Mister Morgen threw the numbers around on the chalkboard. When he got to the four, he said, "Sixteen places, very good. Very good, indeed. Anyone want to challenge? No? Anyone want to have a stab at the last one?"

Hiro raised his hand, and Craig, so near to the focal point, was back to the size and weight he had reached when he was about eight years of age.

"Hiro?"

"I did the last one first," Hiro admitted. "And when I graphed the scream, I thought it would have ever larger curves, but it was only one curve. Did I do something wrong?"

"Let's see," Morgen said and drew a quick graph on the board, filling in specific points until he had the scream drawn out mathematically, if not graphically. It actually ended up looking similar to the line he had drawn when he had been startled by the sound of the scream. Despite, or because of, his blindness, he said, "Now, that looks exactly like what I heard." He scratched his chin thoughtfully. "Good. Very good. You've all done well. Everyone gets an A for the day."

Harold raised his hand.

"Yes, Harold, even you," said Mister Morgen, to which Harold gave out a loud hoot. "You did learn something, right?" Morgen asked the yelling boy.

"I did, sir."

"See there, that's why we're in school after all. It's not to find out what we already know, but to get beyond what we already know. Right, Craig?"

Every eye in the class turned to look at the desk where Craig sat, only to find he had disappeared completely.

"No Craig, huh?" asked Mister Morgen.

Those who weren't dazed and confused at how the pupil had made himself invisible or plain gone answered, "No."

Mister Morgen announced his verdict: "In that case, everyone gets an A, except him. If any of you see him around, tell him I grade on his math work, not his appearance—or lack thereof."

Hiro turned to Mister Morgen and said, "Hey, he did loan me a pencil before he left. Does that count for anything?"

"Sure," laughed Morgen. "Loaning a pencil is at least two percent or less of your final grade. Anyway, homework this week is—"

He was interrupted by a few groans.

"You should always let your teacher finish. I was going to say your homework is canceled, but from the sound of it, you need more, so let's do pages one thousand two hundred and twenty-two through one thousand two hundred and thirty-four."

Those who had groaned were then hit over their heads with

various objects, including heavy textbooks. The only comfort they had then was their A grade for the day. The bell rang and the students left the classroom, some massaging welts, others wondering how they might make a clean getaway next time, like an ever-contracting pupil.

Djonny traveled down to the ground floor for his next class. He took the nearest stairs and was surprised to find a girl on the landing between levels. He had seen her before, though never quite the way he saw her now. He recognized her reddish-brown hair with its large curls, her slender legs, and her serious mouth, which was curved down in fright for obvious reason.

She was shivering and trying her best to hide herself against the bare wall. The wall gave her no protection, and Djonny could see she was ashamed to be without any clothes except her underwear. He thought she should be modeling something other than brick walls and stairwells, but he couldn't bring himself to say so.

She looked at him looking at her. As much to him as to herself, she said, "This must be a nightmare. I need to wake up. Oh, please, wake up." Her voice was as sweet as he expected.

Djonny couldn't help but contradict her. "It's my dream . . . it's my . . . fantasy."

Confusing her sense of propriety and sending her thoughts in abject directions, Djonny took his jacket off. She lurched back toward the wall, expecting something else, but was surprised when Djonny wrapped the jacket gently around her. He left her the music device and even showed her its potential by thumbing it to queue up, "Until you . . . get your clothes . . . unless you want to play supermodel forever." He finished with a friendly nod and a smile.

He walked away as instrumental runway music continued. Happy with his chivalrous self, Djonny hardly cared that by giving her his volume, he was now muted.

8. No Coffee Mug

"This is a general announcement," said the voice on the intercom. "Djonny DeSoto will be fighting Mick Jocctyn right after school. If you don't feel like seeing it live, we'll post it on the school website later. In an unrelated and completely separate vein: Shane Hicks, you need to report to the principal's office immediately."

Djonny wasn't happy hearing the announcement of his impending fight with the psycho boy. But he wasn't terribly surprised, either. The news was bound to travel the school in the form of gossip and was sure to be the hot topic of the day. There was no way of stopping the gossip any more than there was a way of stopping lovers from loving love songs.

Then again, considering Mick's previous note sent by messenger, Djonny thought perhaps this was just another of the psycho's advertising methods. Was he really so relentless?

The classroom Djonny went to next had its own sounds coming from somewhere within. Whether these were melodious or nerve-grating, lovely or loveless, was a matter of taste. Anyone could give their opinion of the good or bad time the English teacher was trying to convey.

As the students jostled through the door, Djonny heard the familiar sound of his friend, Kevin Boseman, skateboarding through the halls. Kevin came speeding up and hopped off his board. "This better be boring, or else I'm ditching."

Someone near Kevin said, "What would you do instead?"

"I'll go home and do chores, I swear."

"Isn't it, like, against the rules to skate in the hallways?" someone else asked.

"It's only against the rules if someone sees you doing it."

Djonny might have argued that, but he was presently without voice.

"Oh, that's right," yet another student said.

They all jogged shoulders getting in the noisy room. A movie was showing on a large screen above the teacher's head, while the sound system continued playing the thrashing sounds Djonny had heard from the hallway. The two systems battled for attention. The teacher seemed oblivious to this as she lectured. Her corpulent body did not move from the chair in which she was stationed. Around her neck was a loop of what appeared to be meatballs on a string. The meatballs looked soggy and heavy, weighing against her shirt and chest.

As the teacher spoke, she brought the necklace to her mouth and bit into one of the meatballs. It didn't slow her talking. The sound system behind her fell silent between songs, and everyone was able to catch the gist of her lecture as they also caught seats.

". . . or should we say that the cycle of stimulus-internalization-response is defined by our environment?" she drawled on. "For such is the articulation of Mustaine in his essay on the frets of syndrome. Oh, how I wish I was a little girl again, thrashing through the violets. That's probably my point. If modifiers were to pluck you from the stem, you could no more see yourself than they could *see* themselves. Lack of them throws us into a kind of magical bumfuzzling, where colors of the flowers could become the flowers themselves. Anything with a name becomes solid, even substantial, despite its wispy, incorporeal nature. Why try to disguise adverbs as nouns? Did they wish for an upgrade? Did they petition for higher social standing? I say, 'Nay.'"

And so she carried on this way while all of the distractions whirled about her. She paid no more attention to the distractions than she did to the words streaming monotonously from her mouth. It was as if she were reliving a series of stone-dead and stone-deaf freedom rally musings.

The unfortunate part of this was the disconnect between her intellectual ramblings and her own ability to comprehend them. This fact was not lost on her audience, leaving some to consider the old adage of listening being more important than speaking since there were two ears and only one mouth. Her students wondered how to let her know; it was impossible to interrupt her, especially when the music kicked in to heavier stuff.

Despite the deafening atmosphere, the teacher's aide insisted on calling out the roll. Djonny, like many, raised his hand when his name was called. At one point, the aide called out Mick's name. There was a distinct, "Here!" but when Djonny looked around, he saw no sign of the boy. The aide tapped her tablet just as she had done on all the other names, marking Mick present.

Two girls near Djonny with matching ponytails were talking back and forth.

"She is so brilliant, isn't she?"

"How can she know so much?"

Djonny was fairly certain the girls weren't talking about the teacher's aide.

Near the door, a digital picture frame shifted slowly from pictures of kittens to bunnies to vixens. It was not apparent to Djonny whether these images were on display for the benefit of the faculty or the studious students.

The room would not let Djonny focus on any one thing for very long.

On top of a filing cabinet at the other end of the room was a glass case in which two familiar tree limbs crossed. Djonny had seen the same kind of sheered limbs at the pet store earlier. Two tree frogs hopped from one limb to the other, rhythmically and repetitively, as if playing a game. The game ended when one frog hopped too far and smacked his face against the glass.

For a moment, everyone's cell phone ringtone played merrily. Each was lost in the general cacophony, however, so not a single call was answered. The music behind the teacher continued, raucous tones and raspy beats accompanied by lyrics that talked about how to get what you want. The volume on the system must have been turned up to at least twenty. The din battered eardrums and shook the children in their seats. More than one student felt as if the constant vibration in their abdomen was going to cause them to hurl.

On the video screen above the teacher's head, two boys were in the midst of indiscretion, to which some in the class gasped. The teacher kept talking, not sensing that she was subjecting others to torture they did not deserve.

To his left, Djonny heard Kevin say, "This is perfectly boring."

But Djonny hardly noticed. His bored and sleepy head drooped toward the pallet of his desk—and found it. Others in the class did the same. The teacher was so caught up in her monolog that she noticed not a one.

Djonny woke a little while later, feeling incredibly refreshed. The music was still doing its thing, threatening to put everyone to sleep. He wondered if he had the selection on his music device. It could be a powerful tool if he had it.

Stretching, he noticed his arms were bare and remembered loaning his jacket to the girl in the underwear. For a moment, he regretted the decision, then realized she probably needed the jacket more than he did. It was an act of chivalry worthy of losing his power of speech.

The teacher was still in the same position and on a familiar topic. "If I say I'm going to ride a letter, you might ask me which one. If I say I'm going to write a letter, you might again ask me which one, and the possibilities are various. I write without modifiers, and therefore I have no business with consonants or cordials."

Above her head, the moving picture was now one of a pleasant cartoon with large-headed children leaping onto a dog house, running and gliding off the other side.

Just outside the class, noticed by few, Mick watched Djonny.

He better not be trying to get out of our fight, or I'll kill him even deader, Mick thought.

Being surrounded by media bombs, Djonny did not notice his stalker; the vitriol was lost in the in-between.

All around Djonny, others were also waking. Not a one woke without some sort of red mark or cloth pattern or line of drool on their face.

"Isn't it cool how when you wake up from a good school-sleep you have the trophy on your face to prove it?" someone behind Djonny remarked.

Kevin said, "I like yours, Fiona. You have the pattern of your sweater on your cheek. So fashionable."

"Thank you," said Fiona. Her eyelids fluttered, and though it could have been a sign of her waking, Kevin took it as a sign she liked him.

"Isn't it incredible how the teacher can remain on topic so long?" Kevin said. "Does she ever stop?"

Fiona had no insight or answer, so it was left hanging in a rhetorical limbo between them.

The two girls with matching ponytails had an opinion about it, though, and the more vocal of the two snatched at the idea. "It's because she studies. She knows the material better than anyone."

Djonny wasn't so sure about that, but he was in no condition to debate it without his voice. Nor could he tell his favorite joke about the heavyset teacher preferring heavy metal. All he could do was wiggle in his seat uncomfortably.

Out beyond the halls, a chorus of bells rang. Rested boys and girls got up from their chairs and filed toward the door. The ponytailed girls approached the teacher to beg her for homework. Kevin again lauded the tremendous state of dullness in the classroom as he followed goth-girl Pam out the door.

"I was put to sleep like an old, rabid dog," he said with a wide grin. "None of my other classes are nearly this boring."

In front of them, Jared the sport star worried, "I think she's trying to make us all gay."

To which Pam spoke in a voice so low she must have practiced it, "I wish she could make me happy."

Djonny smiled and nodded. Following the crowd wasn't his thing, but at the moment, he did exactly that. He had no voice, no music of his own.

9. Song Ten is Missing?

"Right now, someone might be forgetting you. Better remind them that you're here." The voice on the intercom paused reflectively, and the sound of philosophy squelched through the two hundred and seventeen speakers positioned throughout the building. The voice returned again, adding: "Really though, the only ones who are gone forever are those who choose to be. Wrap your little minds around that, slackers."

Kevin, Pam, and Djonny passed the "hardcore" corner where the young toughs gathered, their heads shorn in different degrees. The host of them were busy pummeling each other with whatever implements of destruction were at hand—sometimes even hands.

One teenage brute had on platform shoes. He touched the ceiling as he stood in those shoes and on the face of another of his number. Many of them thought this was the funniest thing they had seen all day. Their laughter echoed through portions of the school.

Djonny followed Kevin and Pam beyond the hardcore circus. Kevin carried his board under one arm in the same way some boys would carry a book.

Twenty feet behind and out of their sight, Mick followed warily.

One hallway contained the country boys and their healthy-looking girlfriends. They had their own idols, who just so happened to wear the same uniform: ball caps and blue jeans. Their music came from a unit plugged in the wall, a small white thing with lots of power, though the music wasn't being played too loud. Some of the kids sat and told stories while others danced in the center of the hall.

Past that, Djonny and his friends found the alcove where the popular kids had their hangout. The popular kids listened to popular music, and their music came from two speakers permanently mounted above their heads on the wall. As Djonny contemplated the fickle nature of the music and the permanently affixed sound system, Kevin said, "Isn't it cool that everyone has their own corner?"

Pam responded despondently. "I don't feel like I fit in anywhere."

"I feel like I could go to any corner and enjoy their tunes for a while, then move to another corner and hang out with another group for a while," Kevin said. His face was full of the love of life.

"Everyone's music has quality and crap. If you can sift through the crap, you'll find the quality."

"Yeah," Pam agreed, "but if you went to the popular kids' hangout, would you start wearing sweaters? If you went to the hardcore corner, would you start shaving your head? If you went to the country corner, would you get a ball cap that says 'I *am* the horsepower'?"

"Not necessary," Kevin said. "The only uniform I need is my smile and my attitude."

"Pfft," Pam scoffed.

At that moment, Djonny wished he could speak. If he could, he thought he might tell Pam that her divisive attitude proved Kevin's idea true—at least in the reverse. Kevin really could hang with anyone because Kevin was friendly. Pam, on the other hand, needed friends, despite her superior ability to turn people off. Djonny imagined some future day when she would fall through a mirror and end up in a universe of the reverse variety. She would find her mirror self—a girl named Map, or something. Map would be a happy blondie with bright eyes and many friends, enough friends to make Pam envious, hopefully envious enough to change her sad, self-defeating ways.

They turned to find the "maturity" corner, where all the so-called "grownup" kids gathered, many of them sitting on the low wall.

Djonny heard the sounds of U2 coming from a figure in the center of a circle of jealous-eyed boys. He watched the circle split as the singer intoned about wild thoughts escaping.

The girl Djonny had met in the stairwell earlier emerged from amid the crowd. No longer clad only in underwear, she was still as beautiful. He watched as her hips appeared to move the rest of her. If the upper half moved, it was because the hips tilted her. If the long and slender legs moved, it was because the hips propelled them. He saw that her hair was less of a mess than it had been before, though he was undecided as to which version of her hair he liked better. And her lips! He couldn't stop himself from staring at those lips. They were their own unique shape—rare gems in the archeology of lips.

Djonny stared, and her hips propelled her lips forward. He stared, and she grew in his sight, from a faraway dream to a close-up vision. She drew his eye, that was certain. A fine figure sketched, she dislodged herself from his jacket and dropped it in his arms unceremoniously. Djonny had to dislodge himself from the haze she cast over his mind. With her so close, it was difficult to be competent or coherent. Even more difficult to be both at once.

She left him as quickly as she had arrived. No thanks escaped her lips. In fact, she said nothing. He stood mesmerized until the circle of frog-eyed boys curled back in around her, hiding her from sight.

When she was gone from sight, he was again able to see the reality around him. His jacket had been returned to him. But what was that red stain on the collar?

Lipstick!

Shrugging the jacket on, he reached for the music player and caught the residual scent of perfume. The music player was slick, as if coated with lotion. Why would she treat his sacrifice so disrespectfully? He began to wonder if she cared about anything at all. What had she done to his stuff?

Kevin's words pulled him from his musings. "You got presents from Roxie Hill. You're movin' up, my friend."

"What good is she?" Pam said. Her jealousy didn't require a response, so she got none. Kevin just pumped his eyebrows for the melancholy girl.

Searching his playlist for something to say, Djonny noticed there were songs missing from his library. Not only had Roxie got slick and sickly-sweet things on the jacket and made it smell girly, but she had reduced his vocabulary, too.

Djonny felt himself starting to take Pam's side. *What good is she?* Not that he was going to start wearing black lipstick or dark eyeshadow like Pam and her disturbed crowd, but he was seriously on the verge of rethinking his present love crush. Then again, Kevin had just told him her name, which Djonny hadn't known. Now that he knew a name, there was something more intriguing about her. *Roxie.* Did her parents name her Roxie because she was so foxy? No, that couldn't be it. Babies weren't foxy. Cute and cuddly, maybe, but not foxy. Clearly, she had grown into her name.

He needed time to think more about this girl. *What good is she?* He would have to ponder that for some time. He excused himself musically. "Baby, baby, baby, I gotta go . . . I've got places to go and minds to blow."

"See you later," said Kevin.

Pam was morose, as usual. "If there *is* a later."

11. Ten Fingers to Burn

"We need Nivek Ogre, Cevin Key, and Dwayne Rudolph Goettel to come to the principal's office at their earliest convenience; something about a sizable government check—about three hundred and thirty-three thousand for each of you. The custodians would also like to warn everyone about the wax on the floors. You can't see it, but you'll know it's there when you feel yourself slip, slip, slipping away."

The electronics class always smelled faintly toasted. Djonny entered with a trudge in his step—not because of the class, but because of the abuse his jacket had sustained. He brushed peanut skins off the right elbow and scraped with a fingernail at some mustard caked in the teeth of the zipper.

Give them an inch, they throw you a mile, he thought.

Djonny bumped shoulders with someone leaving class as the bell rang. It was no one he knew, though he recognized the face. The hair was long and gnarly, the eyes barely there, and the cleft chin unmistakable. Some people called this guy "Skunk," though Djonny didn't detect any odors out of the ordinary.

Skunk's clothes were baggy, the pants especially so, tied up with a rope for a belt. His feet were barely visible under the baggy hems, but when they became visible, it was apparent that he wore no shoes.

"Excuse me," Djonny said for the second time that day, fully expecting the same abusive treatment he had received earlier. He was surprised at what he got instead.

"Hey man, no problem," Skunk said. "What you doin' right now?"

Djonny looked around the room. "Nothing, yet."

"Solid," drawled Skunk.

"What *you* doin' right now?" Djonny asked back in echo.

Skunk's head wobbled with no apparent control. "Yeah, man, we're gonna go smoke. You wanna come?"

"Why would I?"

"We're going to get high. Don't you want to get high?"

"High? You guys smoke behind the trash bins."

A look of consternation crossed Skunk's face, and he could think of nothing better to say than "Pssh," after which he waved a hand dismissively and padded shoelessly out of the room.

The teacher, Mister Norris, noticed this exchange. "So," he said, "are you and Skunk new friends?"

"It ain't nothing like that . . ."

"Sure, right. *Old* friends."

Djonny stared at Mister Norris with his best you've-got-to-be-kidding eyes. After getting no reaction, he decided to give up. He played a repetitive "Babababababababa . . ." and went to his seat at a worktable.

Each of six tables in the room were topped with the paraphernalia of soldering: silvery solder, flux in little containers that looked deceivingly like lip balm, and of course, soldering irons.

"All of the irons have been preheated," Mister Norris began. "Be careful not to burn yourselves. Today, you'll be constructing your own computers with the parts in the boxes in the center of the tables."

"Wow," said some of the students.

"Cool," said the Johnson brothers, who were seated at the same table as Djonny.

Mister Norris continued, "Each of you should have a pamphlet describing the very basics of electron theory. Study those if you get stumped. Don't even bother asking Mister DeSoto for help; he smokes grass."

Djonny looked up in surprise. He had no idea what was eating at Mister Norris today, but he responded in style. "Get bent . . . and where do you get off? . . . I'll get off somewhere else."

"Enjoy yourselves," Mister Norris said. "I'll be in the teacher's lounge if you need me. *Don't* need me."

"Don't need me . . ." Djonny echoed, aggressively obnoxious.

Mister Norris practically ran for the door, as if afraid of his own voice.

The Johnson brothers, Noah and Isaiah, started rummaging through the boxes before Mister Norris was even out the door. Everybody knew Noah was good with the iron, but Isaiah always overanalyzed everything and so tended to need a lot of help.

Noah started on his project right away, not waiting for his brother and seeming to not want to help. Isaiah continued rummaging, laying out parts in reverse order of assembly. Even though it looked complicated, Djonny admired him for having such a thorough process. Djonny, on the other hand, started slapping things together like he was building a primitive radio device rather than a technological, mathematical marvel.

As they worked, Djonny played the DJ and played some Jimi for them all.

Noah appeared to work faster with the music and even admitted, "Jimi's my favorite."

Isaiah, however, looked dismayed and challenged by the music. Djonny recalled Isaiah once telling him his favorite was Charlie Christian. Unfortunately for him, there was no Charlie Christian in Djonny's library. Not yet, anyway.

They soldiered on in their soldering, even allowing the resistors. Out in the hall, an alarm bell rang. The fire alarm.

"Someone must have pulled it," said Noah, quickly attaching his next inducer.

Isaiah nodded. "Bad kids doing bad things."

Djonny nodded his agreement. As they started out the door with the rest of the class, he said, "They don't know what they're doing . . . bad ones . . . to the fire department, to the police, to the whole system."

"Yeah, but if the system works, they *are* keeping it strong," Noah shot back. "You know, in practice. Like here we are, heading out the door because that's what we're supposed to do when the fire alarm goes off. Good practice."

Suddenly, Djonny had a legitimate concern: *What if someone wasn't doing what they were supposed to during the fire alarm?*

"Look," said Isaiah as they walked outside, "there's the police."

A police cruiser sat at the entrance to the school already, though no actual officers were around it. In the distance, the familiar sound of a fire truck was approaching with its crescendoing siren and commanding horn.

Students gathered in no particular order, even though they knew they were supposed to be in their class groups with their teachers, forming straight lines. The teachers were collected in their own group near the school entrance. Mister Norris was with them, looking as if he was missing his favorite television program. Coach Spunk was there too, towering over Mister Norris, with a comparably ornery face. Miss Orleans was there too, watching Coach Spunk's every move.

Djonny felt an unfriendly bump from behind. Thinking it was Mick trying to start the fight early, he whirled into a defensive stance. It wasn't Mick, but one of Mick's questionable friends.

Isaiah and Noah drew close to Djonny, showing their loyalty. Djonny was glad to have friends like them, but it didn't seem to matter to the strange one who had bumped into him. His eyes were lit with the fires of madness, and his hands went up in a mockery of Djonny's defensive stance. He was a large young man, even larger than Mick, so that Djonny thought at that moment he would prefer to fight Mick rather than this guy. The boy had jeans with holes at the knees and ragged edges where he had walked off the hems. His shoes were filthy and untied. His t-shirt read *Death Overdose*, which fit his crazed mug rather agreeably.

Apparently, Isaiah knew the boy. "Give it up, Penrod, or I'll smash your face in the dirt like I did last week."

Penrod stood up straight, and his face shifted instantly from maniacal to serious. "Don't worry so much, Johnson. I'm not here to fight. Unless you really want to . . . Nah, I'm just kidding." He smiled, and his smile was a death overdose kind of smile—the sort that would suit the dead better than the living. "I'm not here to start anything. I just have a message."

Backing out of his stance, Djonny asked, "A message for me?"

"Right," said Penrod. He did an act of making himself proper before delivering the message, straightening the wrinkles out of his shirt, driving his posture upward to form. "Hello, sir. You are Djonny, I presume. My name is Carl Penrod. I ask you to look at the third-floor window." He paused, looking like a dancing monkey, and pointed dramatically to where Sick Mick was framed by one of the large windows, staring deviously down on the congregated masses.

Sick Mick waved.

Djonny knew it was a show set up purposely for him. Especially when Mick pointed with both hands toward the school entrance. Penrod followed Mick's gaze. "And now," he said, dutiful and sycophantic as a circus-show sidekick, "if you'll cast your eyes on the front doors of the school."

The fire truck was pulling in to the circular drive next to the police car, but that was not what Djonny was supposed to see. For his edutainment, there was another show to behold. Two policemen exited through the school doors with a young man in handcuffs. The young man was none other than Djonny's friend, Sam-O.

Sam-O was bent over like a dog beaten, but his voice carried across the yard. "I didn't do it! I didn't pull the fire alarm! I was framed!" He was sincere, but those who didn't know him couldn't tell. The yard was filled with students' laughter.

The police, followed by Principal Byrd, pushed the cooperative body of the boy into the back seat of the cruiser, where he continued to talk loudly to everyone who wouldn't listen.

Firemen gathered, staring in the police car at the "bad boy." They spoke together for some time—police, fire, and school personnel—until Principal Byrd finally took on the mantle of authority. "It was all a false alarm," he shouted to the students. "You can see what happens to those who pull the fire alarm when there isn't really a fire. Now go back to class!"

Penrod was gone when Djonny and his friends looked away from the action, but Mick was still there in the window, waving as if he was the king of a small country and his serfs were gathered in the courtyard. The majority of these serfs were filing back into the building, tittering with the gossip of the moment. Some few were looking furtively to the borders, planning their escapes, but teachers were all around, and escape for these planners would have to be postponed.

Djonny, Isaiah, and Noah were some of the last to get back inside.

"Why do you suppose that guy has such a devious mind?" Noah asked. "Do you think he was raised that way, or did he come by it from reading spy novels?"

Isaiah had his own theory. "Crazy Carl and Sick Mick. They have to live up to their nicknames. Maintaining the illusion, that's what they're doing."

"Let me answer," Djonny said. "I think it's because . . . if we did an autopsy on his corpse . . . we'd find ordure in his cranial cavity."

They laughed as they made their way back to the electronics classroom.

"So, Isaiah, did you really smash that kid's face in the dirt?" Noah asked.

"Yeah, really, and literally. See, he was flicking my ears in gym. He thought it was so funny hearing me tell him to quit it every time, but then Coach left. I'm pretty sure Coach left on purpose, you know, so I could take care of business. Penrod flicked me in the ear from behind one more time, only I didn't say anything. I mule kicked him right in the diaphragm. He bent over. He couldn't breathe, so I pulled his shirt up over his head and started working his ribs over. He still wasn't breathing, and I couldn't have him die on me, so I let go and he dropped in the dirt face first. His face was still purple after he got his breath back. I think punching him in the ribs made him more purple. After a minute or two, he started breathing again. He didn't touch my ears anymore."

Even though they dragged their feet, wanting Isaiah's story to continue indefinitely and not wanting to arrive back at class too soon, it seemed they got there quickly. Noah held the door for them, ushering them in. "Welcome back to reality-land."

Back at their worktable among the circuit boards and random parts, it wasn't long before Isaiah complained of not being able to hold the circuit board and a transistor at the same time. He was struggling, and his brother Noah was ignoring him, so Djonny set his own project aside and helped him.

"Here," Djonny said, "this clamp is . . . meant to hold it for you."

And as Djonny tried to take the circuit board from Isaiah's hands, he grabbed the soldering iron instead. The pain was as hot as it was instantaneous, at the top of the scale in every conceivable way. His fingers seared red and he dropped the iron on the table. It rolled and made contact with the cardboard box, but Isaiah snatched it up before it could burn the box.

"We'll all burn at your helpful hands, DeSoto," Isaiah warned.

"Throw some water on it," Noah advised absently, his computer nearly finished, his attention riveted there. It appeared to be a grand design.

"It burns!" Djonny said left-handed because his right hand was burned. He hopped from the room and made a running break for the only place he could think to go under the circumstances.

12. In the Absence of Heat

The lunch ladies were wonderfully sympathetic. They hooked Djonny up not only with ice but with a tray full of chocolate milk. It made him feel a bit guilty. Before, he had joked about the ladies wearing hairnets, though none of them had much hair to net. Their generosity increased his guilt. In the past, he'd only heard of how these ladies had helped students out with their problems. Now he knew of it firsthand.

He trudged to a table, shuffled in his low-grade guilt, chained to it, pulling it behind like an iron ball, making it a bigger deal than it was. His guilt, mingled with thoughts of Sam-O, were bringing him down as much as the pain. For a short time, he had the whole lunch room to himself. He sat in the center, not really too sad the place was deserted, wallowing in his guilt all alone.

Soon, his fingers grew numb under the bag of ice, but he didn't want to remove them to test them for pain. His mind was drawn to those age-old questions of the origin of pain: Was it like energy, passed from object to object? Did the hot metal feel pain until it had a finger or two on which to relieve itself? Did the wires in the wall feel pain until they could pass it on to the soldering iron? No one knew; the wires could not be asked. If wires carried pain, they kept the secret to themselves.

Djonny watched through philosophical eyes as other students arrived. The first few were a studious-looking bunch, and they made furtive motions as if they were surprised to see him, surprised to have someone invading their perceived territory. Probably they had done some kind of a speed walk, textbooks clutched tight to their chests as they hurried to snatch up a prime table. Djonny guessed at this. He nursed his fingers, rubbing them lightly with the ice bag, considering the early crowd. One of them considered him back.

She was a tall girl with not a round area on her body. Her hair was blondish, tied up behind her head in a tail of some sort. Rooster, perhaps. Or possibly pony. Regardless of what animal the tail represented, the result made her head appear even more stick-like on her long frame. To top it, she had somehow got her bangs shortened and, by perfect product application, stuck the bangs nearly straight up in the air.

Not satisfied to gaze at Djonny, she told him, "Hey, you look kind of familiar."

Prepared for insults, Djonny fumbled with his device and

replied. "I think you got hairspray in your eyes."

Her head reared back in disgust and she stepped away from him. Her friends, having heard the conversation and obviously noticing his graffito, grabbed her, tugging her by her clothes, eyeing Djonny from the dubiously defensive position behind the girl's post-like body.

From somewhere beyond their suspicious eyes, the intercom clicked on to dispense more advice: "Remember, children, not to let abstracts confound you. You can't buy a calorie at the store any more than you can buy a mile. Both are methods of measurement and only exist within your mind. Enjoy your lunch."

Djonny let the words sink in, realizing they had spoken to the very question he'd been pondering. Pain wasn't real at all. It was an abstract—a notion—and it didn't exist, except in his mind. Pain was only the body's way of measuring the activity it required to repair itself. The greater the amount of required repair, the greater the pain.

Measurement. Pain. Abstract ideas.

Djonny opened another chocolate milk and stuffed a straw in it. Lost in thought, he hardly noticed that many others had come into the lunch room. The post-like girl and her friends were now being surrounded by others vying for space.

Djonny began to sip at his milk when he felt someone slap him hard on the back of the head. The unexpected action caused his head to fly forward and the straw to jam in the back of his throat. He instinctively pushed his head back and tested the strength of his threads as he voiced his pain. His mouth tried to open against the seeling strands.

There it was: the pain. It was unreal.

In his haste to scream out, Djonny breathed in some liquid. He coughed behind his closed lips as his lungs tried to rid themselves of the foreign substance. His eyes began to tear up, but he refused to hide the tears and looked around for his tormentor. Or was it tormentors? He wondered this as he caught sight of Ayden, a rough, red-headed boy who liked to tease. He and his buddies were all huddled together and laughing about something. Djonny assumed he knew what that something was.

Ayden looked in Djonny's direction, a malicious humor in his green eyes.

Djonny sighed and turned away. His coughing slowly subsided. The milk came out of his lungs, and soon enough he was breathing normally. Except for the mineral taste in his mouth and the feeling of corporeality being measured in his throat and at his fingertips, he felt the same as ever.

Another student came up to him, trying to be casual, attempting in vain to gain no attention. The attempt would never work. Everyone knew who he was and who he wanted to be. His name was Rascler, and he tended to rub most people the wrong way. Rascler was a dealer. He was probably Skunk's supplier. If Skunk was going to get high from cooking some unknown recipe today, it was most likely Rascler he'd paid for the ingredients.

Rascler looked out of his greasy hair at Djonny.

Djonny stared back.

Hidden in the pockets of his trench coat, Rascler's hands jingled through what sounded like a heavy load of change. His lips moved in the slightest way, as if he were counting the change by the feel of the coins, or perhaps rehearsing a new approach to pushing his illicit wares.

Rascler's words finally came, indicating both possibilities. "Hey, Djonny. You got any change? I need some food from the machines." He nodded in the direction of the endlessly revolving soda can projected over the soda vendor in an oversized hologram.

Smiling, Djonny said, "Only the rich ever beg . . ."

"I'm not *rich!*" Rascler said, emphasizing the last word as if it were a racial slur. One of his hands dropped the change and popped out of the pocket. He shook it at Djonny, the index finger extended like a magic wand ready to throw curses. His mouth threw the threat of curses instead. "If you ever call me that again, I'll make sure you get expelled."

Djonny shrugged. He touched his graffitoed arm with one hand and with the other said, "Today's alright by me . . ."

Rascler's eyes slipped thin and wary. He looked around the room. Not seeing Mick anywhere, he felt it safe enough to say, "So you have business with Crazy Mick? You look crazy enough to deal with him. He'll eat you up and spit you out, boy. See you later—six feet under." With that, he shuffled away, warily scanning the crowd.

Djonny could only shake his head. How could Rascler be looking forward to a career in creating mental illness if he was so afraid of psychos?

The taste of blood was nearly gone, though there was still a stinging sensation at the roof of his mouth in the back. He tried another sip of chocolate. It felt smooth against his wound.

A burst of laughter came from the crowd at the next table. Jill Renee was there, telling jokes. She did that all the time. Like Rascler, she was feeling her way around a potential life career. Unlike Rascler, she actually drew people to her. All for good reason, since Jill Renee was *ha-ha-hee-hee-larious*. She could make your sides ache without using her knuckles. She was no bruiser, anyway. She was a soft and dainty little dark-skinned girl who felt true pleasure in making others laugh.

She threw her fans a one-liner: "Why did the chicken cross the road?"

Someone in her audience moaned.

"No, no, follow me here. The chicken crossed to get to the other side. Okay? Now that you've got the basics, I'm going to take it up a notch. Got it?"

She stood on her chair to give her audience more of a show. Her hands moved expertly with each word.

"Now, two chickens are walking down the same road, each on a different side. One looks across at the other, contemplating, and he says, 'Do you think I should cross to get to the other side?' His friend looks at him and says, 'Why cross? You're already on the other side.'"

The crowd was enthralled. She launched into another: "Three men are killed in a car accident. They meet at the pearly gates of heaven, and Saint Peter asks them, 'What would you like them to say about you at your funeral?' The first man says, 'I'd like them to say that I was of great service to the world.' The second man nods in agreement and says, 'I'd like them to say that I was a great, caring father.' The third man has had time to think about it, and he says, 'I'd like them to say, "Hey, he's moving!"'"

Jill Renee hardly let the kids get laughing before she gave them more. Holding her hands up to demand calm, she said, "Here's another one, in the other direction: So, three men get killed in a gunfight and they go to Hell. The Devil tells them they can get their lives back if they can give him a task he can't accomplish. The first man tells him to fly to the moon. On bat wings, the Devil flies to the moon and comes back. He grabs the man and thrusts him into the fire. The second man tells the Devil to kiss a nun and make her like it. The Devil smiles, pulls a nun out of the fires of Hell (where she's been for some time), kisses her, and she squeals in delight. The second man throws his hands in the air and throws himself into the fire. The third man has had time to think about it, but while he's thinking, he passes gas. He gets an idea right away and tells the Devil, 'Kiss that fart and paint it green.' So the Devil gives him his life back."

The gathered crowd burst into laughter. It took them a while to calm down enough for Jill Renee to begin again. Her next joke came, and Djonny listened closely: "What do you call a zucchini that gets stepped on?"

Some dutiful personage asked back, "What?"

To which Jill Renee replied, "Squash."

The crowd cracked up. Djonny nodded. The joke wasn't even all that funny, but Jill Renee's delivery was absolutely perfect.

She swung expertly into the next one: "What does a rabbit call a zucchini that gets stepped on?"

"Squash," someone guessed.

"No, 'lunch.'" More laughter. She was really wowing the crowd now, and the crowd was growing.

"Okay, what do you call a zucchini on your front porch?"

The same dutiful voice asked, "What?"

Jill Renee paused a moment for impact and then said, "Your neighbor's."

Most laughed, but a few of the members of her audience were a little stumped at that. "'Cause it sure ain't yours," she explained.

More laughter followed her well-crafted explanation. Djonny could imagine her on a stage later in life, doing the same thing with a "mature" audience who should presumably know more about such things. He snickered at his own joke.

Jill Renee heard him and looked in his direction. "You're not really that slow, are you?"

To his dismay, the crowd thought that was a rather funny observation.

Djonny found his menus and scrolled through to find: "What's the difference between a raven and a writing desk?"

Leaping to the challenge, Jill Renee answered wittily, "About seventeen letters, I think."

Her crowd loved it, laughing until their faces hurt. Djonny stood and bowed to her, and a moment later, she bowed back.

"It looks like all you're doing there is drinking, but if you have any more one-liners, you let me know, okay Mister Music?"

"Drinking . . ." Djonny said. "Sounds perfect . . . perfectly ponderous to me."

Jill Renee returned to her audience and started in on some more

62

hilarity.

Djonny, however, had to leave. His next class was gym, and it was on the other end of the campus. He left his tray, his ice, and the remainder of his chocolate milk on the table and exited the lunch room.

Jill Renee certainly had a gift. She made people happy. She had filled Djonny with some measure of joy; he could testify. She was a healer. A shaman. Or should it be sha-woman? It sounded perfectly absurd to his chocolate milk mind.

Regardless of what Jill Renee might be called to identify her spiritual gift, she had managed to fill some of Djonny's emptiness, and that was super-alright with him.

13. Break Down

"Coach Spunk would like to announce that all seventh graders need to delouse before gym. No exceptions. Joan J. of the ninth grade, just call it love. Milo A. of the eighth grade, you have overdue library books. And Amanda G. of the seventh grade, your mom brought your lunch; it's here at the main office. Smells delicious, though, so you better hurry if you want it."

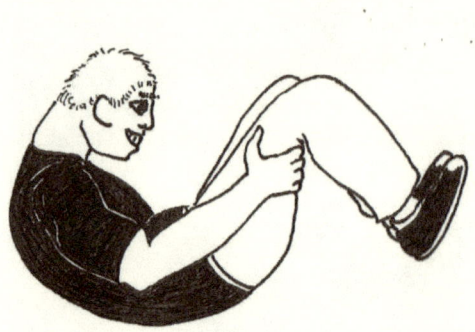

Beto was there in gym class at his usual sport. The grippy-slick wooden floors of the bucketball court were his dance arena, and Beto had the skills to make the dance moves look easy. Try them yourself, as Djonny had many times, and find out how really difficult they were. Find out how weak your abdominal muscles might be when you're trying to hold your legs out parallel to the ground in a mock push-up position.

Djonny found Beto throwing his body around in spins and flips, the beat apparent by his moves, but otherwise not audible. Beto had the music in his head.

Clapping, Djonny got Beto's attention. He slid up to Beto laterally to show him the display of his music device. There were a few selections Beto liked. He pointed at one that Djonny also happened to like, so Djonny started it for him. The beat was perfect for breakdancing, and Beto took off like a manic puppet suddenly finding itself free of its strings.

The boys playing bucketball stopped what they were doing when they heard the music and came over to watch.

"Wow!" one said, and the others echoed him.

They all began to try some of Beto's moves, mimicking him as he went. They weren't as good, but they were having fun with it anyway.

Soon, it looked as if all they would do that day in gym class was dance, but Coach Spunk showed up at the other end of the gymnasium and began setting up weights on the weight benches so that everybody knew today was weight training day.

The hip-hop music ended, and everyone began asking Djonny for another. He picked one called "In 3s," and Beto had a time keeping up with the changes. The song started out fast, slowed to a funky beat in the middle, then ramped up and slowed again. Beto made it look as if the music was in him, an essential part of his soul.

Coach Spunk snuck up behind the gathered crowd of boys, and when the song ended, he clapped the loudest and whistled as if they were all far away from him.

The major problem with Coach Spunk was that no one could ever tell if he was serious or joking. He had a sense of humor, for sure, but his facial expression was always on the "pissed" side. It was as if he could throw down an angry tantrum at the slightest provocation, and no amount of jocularity would distract him when the time came.

"Alright, pansies," Spunk began, "now that you've had your warm-up, it's time to show your mama she didn't waste her time birthing you. Anyone have a problem with weight training today? No? Good. I'd hate to have to fold you in half and mail you home to your mama. That would be embarrassing. Now get to the benches."

Everyone scurried to the opposite side of the gym, coupling up in their usual pairings, finding their friends so they wouldn't get stuck with a spotter who couldn't handle the weight they were sure they could lift. Of course, many of them wanted Harold as their friend; he lifted weights as effortlessly as Beto channeled a beat.

Beto and Djonny teamed up, just as they wanted. Coach Spunk looked at the boys, and his expression changed briefly from piss to pity. He blew air from his mouth in what amounted to a manly sigh. "Pffff." His eyes narrowed, and he settled into his usual coaching stance: legs stretched slightly apart, arms crossed in front of his thick chest, and head tilted slightly forward to bellow commands more forcefully.

"Today, we will be doing—"

"Who's we?" mumbled Harold.

Spunk turned his attention toward Harold without breaking his stance.

Harold was too daft to know danger when it shouted in his face, so he kept talking. "I've just never seen you lift weights."

"What!?"

"I said—"

"I heard what you said, boy. And I believe you got kicked in the head by a horse a long time—"

"Mule," Harold corrected, nodding energetically and wide-eyed as if it was a happy memory.

Though several of the boys laughed, Coach Spunk did not. Instead, he acted as if the offending statements were piling up before him like so much manure. He shook his head to clear it and began again, this time more calmly, trying to keep his professional composure.

"Today, we will be doing circuit training. For those of you who haven't done it before, this means a small amount of weight at each station, repetitions of at least ten, and moving quickly to the next station. Improving your strength in all muscle groups will improve your tone and ability to build specific muscles."

Spunk looked thoughtfully at Harold. The man's lip curled up on one end before he continued. "Since some of you feel the need to challenge me, I will be adding myself to the circuit. If you are too slow, and you're ahead of me, I will personally crush you with whatever weights are in my hand, and then I will personally call your mama to tell her how you died from being too slow."

One joker at the other end started lifting. The weights clanked together at each repetition.

"I didn't say go!" Coach Spunk bellowed. "Did I say go?"

"Nooo," said a few of the boys. The premature lifter racked his weights.

"Alright, boys. Bootlicking. Not necessary. Now GO!"

Spunk raced to an empty bench and madly threw out ten reps, all the while laughing like a playful child. He immediately caught up to the next boys in line, who were only in the middle of their counting. Lifting the boy off the bench, Spunk set him and his weights down on top of his spotter—then added two 45s to the top of the pile.

"Get out of that, fairies. Ha!"

Harold and his partner were through with each of their sets, and they were next after Coach Spunk, so the boys happily vacated, leaving an empty space. They eyed Spunk warily as they moved to the next station: the squat rack. Others along the line sensed the tension mounting as they counted rapidly for themselves and cheated for others, skipping numbers here and there.

Spunk laughed all the harder as he finished his set and moved into the preacher curl, just one station behind Harold. "I'm getting closer," Spunk taunted.

Harold began to sweat. His hands began to slip on the metal bar. "More chalk," he demanded.

Spunk jumped up from the preacher bench just as Harold counted, "Ten."

Spunk laughed maniacally. He was having too much fun abusing all the tense minds. Sliding right in where Harold left off, he did all of his squats while staring in Harold's direction. The sweat began to pour off of Harold as if he had been soaked with a hose.

While Coach Spunk's attention was on Harold, one of the other pairs of teenage boys snuck ahead around Djonny and Beto. One of them was the boy who drove to junior high. Djonny could never recall his name because it was so foreign to him. Mahorajib, or Morfalalaway, or something like that.

It didn't matter what his name was—everyone knew who he was. He was the only boy in the whole school with a mustache, sideburns, and a driver's license. Most people couldn't pronounce his name and just called him "Mustache." He was there because he had a difficult time finishing anything.

At the same moment Spunk was approaching Harold menacingly, Mustache quit his own workout and backed away. "I just can't handle this anymore.," he said, bowing out of the competition.

His partner threw his hands in the air and said, "I can't do it all myself," obviously disturbed that he was forced to do the same.

If Spunk saw the two step out of the line of exercise stations, he made no motion to indicate he did. Instead, he threw Harold to the ground and stepped on top of him as if their relationship was not teacher and student but hunter and game.

Spunk bounced on the large child, snarling his words. "See, Harold? I told you I'd crush you. Today is the day you learn not to tempt your superiors."

With each bounce, Harold giggled. The giggles grew louder when

Spunk drove his heels in. With each bounce, Harold got closer to getting the words out. "Oguh . . . oguh . . . oguh . . . ogay . . . ogay. Okay! Stop! You're gonna make me pee. Get off!"

Spunk acquiesced. His face was a thick mixture of frustration and amazement. In his habitual sportsman way, he stretched a hand out to help Harold up. Harold took the offering and hoisted himself upright.

The other teams had stopped what they were doing to watch the show of Spunk using Harold as a trampoline. Djonny and Beto, however, kept going. Still amazed by Harold's resilience, Spunk didn't bother to watch as Djonny and Beto were the only ones to actually finish the circuit.

As if it were a sign of the end of times, there was a rumble from within the earth. Everyone in the class looked toward Djonny and Beto, thinking they had dropped a weight, but it was obvious they hadn't since there were no loose weights on the floor anywhere near them.

"I guess I didn't know . . . I was so strong," Djonny said, shrugging his shoulders.

Beto smiled his big cheesy smile and said, "I knew I was."

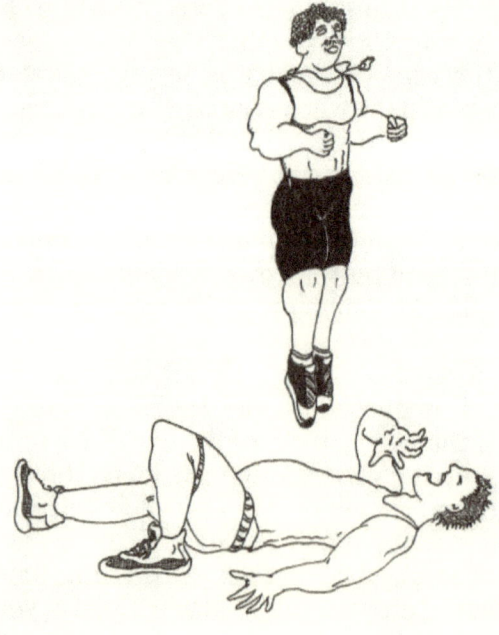

14. Fork, Spork, Splork

The intercom clicked on, and the voice made an unpleasant guttural hawking noise before saying, "Sorry to interrupt your wonderful time here in your favorite place while doing the most favorite of things, but I've been ordered to tell you by an unnamed teacher that if you don't study history, you'll be doomed to repeat it. I think that means you'll have to retake the course, but you can divine your own meaning."

At lunch, Djonny went through the line and loaded his tray with every protein imaginable. He had eggs and bacon, cheese and whey, wheat and hemp—even poultry and fish. He got some more chocolate milk, but he filled it with the hemp, wheat, and whey so that it was more protein blend than sugary snack. After breaking down the muscles, he needed to rebuild.

Djonny saw Roxie sitting with a group of girls and made a beeline for the table. Even though the unspoken rule dictated anyone who didn't normally sit at a particular table should ask permission before doing so, Djonny sat down without asking. No one at Roxie's table seemed to mind. They carried on without protest, enjoying their conversations as if he had always been one of their crowd.

Two tables over, Kay and her friends were having a lively conversation. Djonny heard none of it; he was too focused on Roxie.

Roxie looked at him with a puzzled expression. "Weren't you in first lunch?"

"How would you know?"

She shrugged. "I just do."

"Have you been . . . watching me?" he asked.

Roxie smiled slightly. "I wouldn't say 'watching.' More like 'noticing.' I've been *noticing* you." She bit into a potato finger and let Djonny ponder the semantics of her admission.

"Better to be noticed than . . . invisible."

"You are visible, even audible. But I never noticed you before. I've been trying to figure that out all day."

Djonny stuffed a straw into his special protein mix. "I learned your name today," he said.

Roxie looked down at the table. "I learned yours today too."

Djonny stuck the straw between his seeled lips. As he drank, he saw Ayden creeping up behind him. The step was stealthy and the arm was outstretched, ready to slap. The back of Djonny's head was clearly such a tempting target that Ayden was ready to strike again.

This time, Djonny was prepared. He ducked around the imminent slap, grabbed a fork from someone else's plate, spun out of his seat, and drove the fork in the side of Ayden's leg with a *splork* sound. It stuck in the flesh, and Ayden fell backward, crying out in shock and pain.

Djonny considered kicking the fork even further into the boy's leg but decided that was not his style. Someone more vicious might have acted on the impulse, but instead Djonny snatched up some napkins from the same random person's tray and brought them to Ayden. He pulled the fork out of the downed boy's leg, threw the fork away, and handed him the napkins.

"Put a stop to the bleeding," Djonny said. "You're not dying."

"I didn't think I was dying!" Ayden spat. He accepted the napkins anyway and applied them to his leg with pressure.

"Why do you tease me the way you do?" Djonny asked.

Ayden said nothing. His head drooped, and his lips got tight. He wouldn't look Djonny in the eyes.

"We could be friends," Djonny said.

Ayden made a doubtful face, still not looking at Djonny.

"At least we could . . . cause trouble together," Djonny offered.

Now Ayden was attentive. He looked up from his bloody napkins to see if he could catch whatever notion was in Djonny's mind. Not sure of what he'd found, he asked, "What are you talking about?"

"Curious? Are you?"

"Of course," Ayden said. "Why wouldn't I be?"

"Some people wouldn't."

"Yeah." Ayden nodded. "Boring people."

"I see," said Djonny. "So, you want to know . . . what I have in ma-my-my mind?"

Ayden looked at his wounded leg. "I'm not going anywhere. What are you talking about?"

Djonny turned back to the table of girls. He may not have asked if he could take a seat, but he felt the obligation to do so now. "Can my friend . . . join us?"

"Sure, yeah, that's alright," came a chorus of girls' voices.

Roxie's was the only acceptance Djonny really wanted, but he was glad to get the others' anyway. He made sure there was an empty chair next to him for Ayden, then sat down and resumed sipping on his protein drink.

"I swear I can see you growing," Roxie said, and Djonny felt a stirring in the general area of his abdomen, like warmth and health had wrapped themselves together behind his aphrodisiac jacket to share the space.

"So what's your idea?" Ayden asked, but Djonny was having a difficult time concentrating. His focus was elsewhere. He looked up at the ceiling, a tactic that helped him think more clearly. Ayden grew tired of waiting for a response and suggested, "Maybe you want to get revenge on the guy who gave you stitches in your lip?"

Djonny chuckled lightly. "Actually . . . I need more art," he said, pointing at the graffito on his jacket. Then he pointed at other places. "Here, here, and here."

"You might ruin your jacket," Ayden warned.

"It *is* a nice jacket," Roxie agreed.

"I'm sure I could get another one," Djonny said, "but I don't have time today . . . to go get one. I have to finish this now."

"Wait," Ayden said. "I think I understand what you're thinking. It might not work, you know? There are lame crazies and sick crazies and wannabe crazies and stupid crazies. Mick's the sick kind of crazy. He might not care."

"A chance I'm willing to take," Djonny said.

One of Roxie's friends leaned toward Ayden. "And which kind of crazy are you?" she asked.

If Ayden heard, he ignored her and didn't answer the question, dabbing at his clotting instead.

"Alright, count me in," Ayden said. "I know a couple of people who have paint pens. And I can draw some."

"Good," said Djonny. "Can we beg, borrow, and steal?"

"Hey, I know someone who can draw signs like that too," Roxie offered, pointing at the paint on Djonny's jacket.

"Excellent," Djonny said loudly and melodically. Then, more quietly, he added, "Now we need a secret place to conduct our affairs."

"I can help with that too," Roxie added with a playful smile.

"I'm totally intrigued," Djonny said.

"Me too," said Ayden, obviously puzzled.

Everyone at the table laughed except for Djonny. He finished his lunch thoughtfully, pleased by his newfound friends.

15. Pop Rocks? Are You Sure?

"Contrary to popular rumors, those attending summer school still have to come back in the fall. Billy Gretsch, you and your guitar are wanted in the counseling center. All students entering the center must have replication identification cards ready. Does anyone wish school was from dusk 'til dawn?"

In Djonny's next class, there was an interesting arrangement between the teacher and the students. The students all wanted to be there; in fact, some never left. They were studious and wanted to learn. Book savvy and computer literate, they carried on their own system of learning. Their teacher, one Señor Cajahuanca—first name Willy—accepted his role as advice giver, rarely participating except on those occasions when the students had specific obstacles to their training.

Today, the class had received a cartload of computers from electronics that needed the initial boot.

Djonny watched with pride as his creation came back to him. It wasn't as perfect as Isaiah's or as finished as Noah's, but it was still something he had begun and so was glad to finish. Unlike others in the class, he took his time placing the kernel and watching it grow.

Some of the nerds got done in lightning speed. They quit after only a few minutes and after all the basics were there. Djonny, however, took his time and added features. As he did this, he had a sensation of being distant from his creation, like God staring down at the Milky Way. Were all things in place? Was it all functional?

While he was still piling on the excess, the other boys were moving on to their preferred activities—some to the videos, others to the messenger system. Within the school were two systems, placed there by the staff long ago: audio and visual. Another system was also introduced long ago. Its main reason for being was so the students could circumvent the first two systems. So, they devised and designed the messenger system. The audio and visual systems, dubbed "The Schoolnet," were easily tapped by the brighter students and used by student and staff alike, though it was unclear how many of the staff actually knew that the students had tapped into the system.

On any given day, the brighter students—or, more specifically, the students in this very room—would be watching and listening and reporting what they witnessed. For the juicier information, money sometimes changed hands. The messengers, of course, helped relay the information and channel the funds.

Djonny was busy recreating a music format on his computer when he overheard, "Fire on level three!" and looked up from his work to see who said it. It was Darrel Cox, a scrawny young man who looked like he might have trouble pushing an office chair around even if it had wheels—the same Darrel Cox who had greeted him on his arrival at school that morning.

Darrel's fingers were lightning fast at the keyboard, proving his speed as he typed commands and reported the fire to the others.

"Hey," Djonny said, "can I ride on your feed?"

Darrel replied without looking at Djonny. "Just don't tie on anything slower than tetragigapixel, or I'll have to forcefully bump you."

"Hexagiga . . ." Djonny said with a crooked smile.

The picture came up on Djonny's new screen, and he recognized the space. "Smoking? In there?" he asked to anyone who would listen.

"Right," Darrel said, and a few others agreed. "And I'll bet the fire was intentionally started."

"No way," Djonny said playfully.

From the corner came two voices in unison: "Not our son."

The joke earned them a few snickers.

Djonny shifted gears and decided to wonder out loud. "What is the point of the smoking toilet?"

"Good question," someone commented, and they all watched as four boys exited the room, laughing and waving thick smoke out of their faces.

"New question," one boy said, addressing Darrel. "Can we isolate the fire sprinkler system on that level to put out the fire and give those boys a soak?"

"Another good question," Darrel conceded. He typed for a second and followed with, "Let me see what can and can't be done." Half a second later, he was sporting a satisfied smile. "Yeah, watch and learn, gentlemen."

On Djonny's screen, the overhead sprinklers came on suddenly, and the boys found their sprint right away. The camera view followed them, as did the sprinklers. The boys were of the long-haired variety, and soon their hair was sticking to their faces under the downpour. They spat drips out of their mouths and tried in vain to keep their hair from plastering in front of their eyes. They kept running, attempting to outrun the sprinklers, though they couldn't be so obtuse as to think they were faster than gravity. Or so Djonny thought.

As the four boys—who now looked very much like wet cats—made it to level two and sprinted out of the stairwell, dodging left and right, they were stopped by a messenger.

The messenger was one of the best Djonny had ever seen in action. He was the same short red-headed boy Djonny had seen earlier. Despite the messenger's reputation as a professional, someone in the classroom said, "I hope his message isn't on paper."

"Paper?" said someone else. "Not Reese. Watch."

To his credit, Reese produced a disposable razor and began to shave the red hair from his own head. The boys in the wet hallway were mesmerized—too mesmerized to keep running. Reese was giving himself a mohawk right in front of them. When he was done shaving in the fire sprinkler water, he turned his head to one side.

"Zoom in! Zoom in!" some of the class demanded.

Darrel switched from camera to camera until he had the right angle, and then he obliged the voices by focusing the shot. Inscribed on Reese's head above the left ear, in what looked like a permanent tattoo, were the words: *Feel like you've been left out in the rain?*

The smoker boys looked even more amazed—a sentiment mirrored on the faces of those watching from the remote classroom. One young man was not so mesmerized that he couldn't speak. "How did he get that message *under* his hair?" he asked.

"Wait a second," said another. "Look!"

Reese turned his head to display the other shaved side, which bore more tattooed words: *Go back and make it right.*

"Whoa," said Darrel.

"Yeah, he knew your mind," Djonny pointed out.

"Let it work. Let it work," demanded some.

"Alright, I will," Darrel said. "Only let's see if they go back."

All eyes were on the screens. Sure enough, the long-haired boys went back up the flight of stairs toward the still-smoking room. Darrel continued the pattering pattern and flooded the smoking space to put the fire out. Moments later, the wet-haired boys came out. When the fire sprinklers did not follow them, they looked relieved. They spun their heads energetically and whipped the water out of their hair. Water halos spread in four different directions.

Darrel switched the cameras off. "I think we owe them the reward of privacy. At least for a few minutes."

Darrel sighed and watched Djonny for a sign. Djonny just gave him the melody of a psychedelic love song.

Darrel looked left and up, as if remembering something. "Hey," he said, "do you want to see some funny video we got last week?"

"Sure enough," Djonny said. "Play it."

Cueing up the previous week, Darrel showed Djonny a section of the school where the shop classes were. He then went to the video. In the wood shop, several young men were busy sawing, routering, and nailing.

The teacher looked over these operations with smug pride written plainly on his face. He offered his advice to the router operator. "Keep it tight against the jig!" he yelled over the loud machines so the router operator could hear him.

Behind them and to their right, another young man was using the table saw, and doing so within the safety zone—though apparently not all of him was in that safety zone. Behind him was a sign with the words: *Watch what you saw*. To the boys in the shop class, it was a safety warning. To Djonny, it looked like a message to replay the video.

The transition was obvious. One moment, the room was in a state of peaceful creation. The next, everyone was running about excitedly, killing power to machines. The boy at the table saw was at one moment calm, and the next jumping away from the saw, digging through the sawdust at the base of the machine. He came up with the treasure: his own finger. Though it was certainly painful and somewhat gruesome, he still showed the severed digit to everyone in the class. The class fell silent; all of the machines were turned off.

One of the fingerless boy's friends approached him and said, "Wow, man, you lost a finger."

The boy nodded seriously. He looked down at the severed finger in his hand, studying it, then studying the place where the finger should have been, a bloody mess being attended briefly by others with first aid kits.

An odd thought seemed to cross his mind, and he smiled at his friend. "Hey, man, high four!"

He held his bloody hand up as an offering, and his friend smacked it happily. The boy continued giving high fours through the crowd as the teacher escorted him from class.

"We have to get you to the emergency room," the teacher said. "Get your finger reattached."

The video ended. "That's tremendous," Djonny said. "Got any others?"

"Hey," said Vince, one of Darrel's close friends, "show him the montage you made."

"I could," Darrel said. "It's something I threw together right after second lunch. This loner found some friends. You might like it."

Djonny watched the monitor and saw his very own scrawny self sitting in the lunch room, sucking on chocolate milk with a bag of ice on his burnt hand. There wasn't a soul near him. He even pitied himself for a moment, feeling the isolation of that large room and the single figure at the center of it.

The lonely scene transitioned into time-lapse, speeded up so that all the children looked like little runts on caffeine racing everywhere, bouncing off of each other, heads and arms shaking spastically as they ate and talked. The motion slowed gradually through double-time, back to normal. Djonny was there again, this time sitting between Roxie and Ayden, surrounded by girls.

"Two lunches, eh?" said Darrel. "You rebel."

"I was hungry," Djonny protested.

"Yeah, I bet you were," Vince burst. "Why's your lip sewn up, anyway?"

"It was . . ." Djonny searched for the right words. "I'm sure . . . it was conscious carnality. Time to show the world . . . the change the music made in me. The change made long ago, not even noticed then, only felt now . . . realized in this superior form."

"Okay, Captain Cryptic," Darrel laughed. "You know what I think. I think you wanted an excuse to show off your vast music collection. How much does it cost to buy all of that music, anyway?"

"It depends. It varies."

"I know, because I have an iPod. A Shuffle."

"They still make those?" Vince teased.

"You can shut up now," Darrel remarked. "Anyway, as I was saying, I have a Shuffle, and I can do the math. You've probably spent upwards of fifty thousand dollars if you have the most recent system, and it's only halfway filled."

Djonny cut in with, "I fail to see the relevance."

"Don't sidestep me. You know better than I do. I'm just making a mathematical observation, that's all. It's a waste of money."

Head tilted to the side, Djonny appeared to consider the possibility.

Vince came to his defense. "It's not wasted at all. He's using it in a way that hasn't really been done before. He's innovative, creative, and contemplative."

With a capture and swift release, Djonny repeated Vince's words back to him: "Innovative . . . Creative . . . Contemplative . . ."

On the second repeat, he played the words with a background of rocking guitars and a backbeat. On the third, he played them with horns and a funk rhythm.

"Alright," Darrel came to the party, "I got it. You win. It's not wasted."

"Skunk is," someone said, and they all looked to the monitors.

There was Skunk, weaving steadily through the lower hallway with his jaw slack, his candy-corn yellow teeth protruding like a feeble animal, his eyes windows on the dead soul. He was *shi-ni-rei*, as the Japanese say. He was tripping in his mind, and nearly tripping on his own bare feet. A couple of those watching laughed at the way Skunk couldn't walk in a straight line and the way he was using the wall to support himself every third step.

From behind him and down the hall, barely noticeable as a human shade, came Pam. She had her usual bad posture, but her face showed an unblinking predatory furtiveness. Her eyes darted everywhere, taking in the entire hallway. She saw no one else; she and Skunk were the only ones in the lower hallway.

Apparently, that was what Pam wanted, because she loped up behind him and leaped in the air. Skunk heard her last footfall and turned his head in time to see her propelling forward, her arms and legs reaching for him. Skunk let out the brief, urgent squeal of prey knowing death has found it.

She caught him when she landed on his back, and her arms gave an animalistic tug strong enough to twist him and hurl him sidelong to the dark corner of the hall. The extra force of the throw took him out of consciousness, which wasn't that much of an accomplishment considering how much of that he really had left.

There in the shadows, Pam thrust her head to the back of Skunk's throat. Through the audio, everyone could hear a violent sucking. In moments, Pam got up from the floor, but Skunk did not, would not, could not. It looked as if all that was left of him was a dried-up worm of a carcass. His juices had all been drained, and he was shriveled beyond recognition. Pam looked rather healthier as she picked up Skunk's dry remains and snuck off, presumably to dispose of them.

"What a trip," someone watching said, and a few in the class laughed.

"It can't be real," Djonny said. "That blood spree."

"Good job, whoever put that together," said Vince.

A few eyes landed accusingly on Darrel, but he denied it. "I didn't make that video. Isn't it happening now?"

"It can't be real. If you didn't, then who did?" Vince asked.

No one in the classroom admitted to anything.

"It makes sense no one wants to own up to it," Darrel said. "You don't make something like that and tell people it's a fake right away. You let it gain momentum, get some word-of-mouth advertising and a few thousand controversial comments. Then you spring it on everyone that it was all a sham—a shrek, bullsh . . . you know."

"Bullsham? Bullshrek?" Vince offered.

Darrel snickered. "Not exactly."

"I made it," Djonny said, to which many in the class groaned. Others congratulated him on his success at the art of film.

"You could've pulled it off," Darrel said. "It's a possibility."

Djonny smiled. "Things seem possible to you because you were recently born."

"I wasn't born yesterday. You could be covering. Maybe you're one of them."

"It would be the last thing you knew."

"Are we talking about birth and death in the same sentence?"

"We're talking about . . . your sentence."

"Good one," Darrel said, swallowing hard in a show of nervousness. "And with your suit of black, your mummified mouth, pale face, and dark hair, you probably *are* one of them. I should have seen it before."

"How did I hide before?"

"Intelligence," Darrel proclaimed after a moment of thought. "Intelligence is the universal disguise."

Everyone had to think about that for a minute. They even considered their own intelligence. Djonny didn't have to think on it much. He knew how it felt to be invisible, and when you were one of the smart ones, you were invisible. That was exactly why Roxie hadn't noticed him before. He had to make some noise, play some music, talk through the voices of the great musicians. Only then did she notice him.

Still, he didn't hold any grudges for the past. Djonny was happy enough with his present audience. He enjoyed being watched. It simply depended on who was watching.

16. Unwind, Rewind

He found her waiting for him. He wondered at the reality of this. All things have their truth, and all things have their illusions. Djonny wondered which side he would see first. The truth, he hoped, would be exactly what he was seeing now.

Her eyes were brighter somehow. Or was he seeing them for the first time? Had those eyes always been so quick to catch the light? Did the light always dance there? He shook his head to clear it and found the perception was not something like dizziness that could be mastered physically. He had to clear this feeling some other way, or accept it.

Roxie reached out with something in her hand as an offering. Her eyes followed him as he approached. When he was close enough, he accepted it. It was a small mp3 player.

"I thought since I lost some of your music earlier you might like this," she said.

"Where did you get it?"

"It's mine. I've had it in my locker for a while, but I haven't used it lately."

"What does it have on it?"

"Girly music," she said and laughed.

"Am I going to regret this?"

"Of course not, silly. Why don't you look through it and see if there's anything you can use?"

Interrupting them from behind came a voice so similar to Pam's that Djonny thought it was her. "Aren't you going to introduce me?"

Roxie's head drooped. "Sorry. Djonny, this is my friend, Toni. Remember I said I knew someone . . ."

"Hello. I'm Djonny. I'm the deejay."

"That's far out," Toni said, staring openly at Djonny's lips, which hadn't moved.

Roxie laughed.

"What?" Toni asked.

"Nothing."

"Ayden . . . isn't here," Djonny said, as if the whole operation hinged on Ayden's presence. He knew it didn't, but he wasn't altogether comfortable with Toni. She had curves like a girl, but there was something not quite right with those curves—and staring at them was not the way to figure out what was so out of balance.

As if to tip the scales herself, Toni asked, "Can I try? Where do you want it?"

"Not here either," Djonny said, looking around.

"Right," Roxie agreed, "I know where."

She led the way, and Djonny followed. Toni came, skipping along beside them.

When they got to the third-floor girl's bathroom, Roxie turned to Djonny as if expecting him to protest.

He eased her worry. "This will do just fine . . . but first things first . . ." He turned to find the nearest security camera, gave it the okay sign, and held the door for Toni and Roxie.

On the other side of the door, Toni pointed at Djonny and said, "I must have stepped into heaven, because you are an angel."

Roxie gave her friend the concerned eyes, but with fire behind them. It was apparent she hadn't seen this side of her friend before. "Keep it cool, Toni," she warned.

"Aah," Toni sighed, "I know what you mean. It is so hot in here." She fanned herself with a flat hand and slid closer to Djonny. "So, now, where do you want it?"

"You have a paint pen?" Roxie asked.

"Oh, ah, ah, ah," Toni panted, "I have more than one." As she reached a hand in her purse, Djonny noticed she was sweating like an athlete at the peak of performance. "I had one in here somewhere." She rummaged through what sounded like endless collections of plastic baubles. The items in her purse clacked together with a rhythm of faux tableau.

"I don't have all day," Djonny argued.

"Your voice sounds so fabulous," Toni said. "I wish I could walk around like a walking jukebox. Oh, here it is." She held the paint pen up and turned toward Djonny and his jacket.

"Where do you want it?" Djonny asked in Toni's voice.

She took a step backward with a confused expression. "That doesn't sound like me at all. What are you trying to do, kill the mood? Where did you find this guy, Roxie? He's so vile."

"Just draw some graffiti on his jacket and we can get out of here," Roxie demanded, growing tired of Toni's weirdness.

Toni slapped the pen into Roxie's hand. "Here. Do it yourself." She took her purse full of plastic collections clacking out the restroom door with her.

When the manic emotions fled out the door with Toni, Djonny made his lips a straight line and crossed his eyes.

"I don't really know her that well," Roxie admitted. "She never seemed that unhinged before."

Djonny nodded. "Something twisted inside that one . . . the mind of a viper . . . in the body of a tractor."

Roxie nearly fell on the floor laughing. Djonny couldn't help laughing himself. Watching each other laugh made them laugh even harder, and they began to wonder if they could ever stop.

Finally, Djonny said, "It hurts . . ." and they managed to calm down.

"We should have brought Ayden instead," Roxie said, wiping a tear from the corner of her eye.

"Wonder where he is . . . I hope he's healthy."

Roxie snorted, almost launching into a new bout of laughter, but managed to hold it in. "His mind is healthier anyway."

A bell rang, and they went for the door. The long-haired rockers Darrel had chased with the fire sprinklers spotted them coming out of the bathroom.

The tallest of the group called out to Djonny. "Hey, man, better be careful coming out of the bathroom like that. You could get soaked."

Djonny responded by playing them some death metal that had nothing to do with fire or water or bathrooms. Djonny didn't really know what the song was about; the "singing" sounded mostly like animalistic growling. But it was received well. The boys started whipping their hair around violently.

"Yeah, cool!" one of them said, recognizing the song. "Dead Reich!"

"Man, I gotta get me a jacket like that," another of the boys said.

Djonny halted the music. "I'll make you one."

"Cool," two of the boys said in unison while the other two grabbed them and forced them down the hall.

Djonny turned to Roxie to say something, but she was already moving away. She waved him on, and the class bell rang.

"We'll get you some more graffiti," Roxie promised as they parted.

Djonny smiled and jogged away, repeating in a pitch-shifted recorded voice, "Where do you . . . Where do you . . . Where do you . . . want it?"

17. Everybody Wants...

"The east relocatable is burning, so all classes once held there will now be held in the swimming pool where the fire can't get you. And more building woes: Being one hundred and sixty-eight years old, the west wing finally succumbed to gravity, so all classes that would've been held there will be held in the unused tennis building. Being one hundred and seventy-seven years old, Missus Fensterwasch, the health teacher, has retired the old-fashioned way by passing away at her desk. She will be buried behind the botany greenhouse. May we observe a moment of silence in her honor?"

French studies was one of Djonny's more whimsical classes. The teacher was a Swedish man, not a Frenchman, the room was set up like an auditorium, and the class was ninety-six percent girls. Djonny was the sole male, aside from the teacher. Before he had met Roxie, it was a great way to speak with the fairer sex.

On this particular day, he was daydreaming of the time when class would be over and he could see and hear and smell Roxie again. She was starting to occupy a great deal of his thoughts, and he was a bit worried it might lead to a four-letter word: love.

Djonny looked around the room. Here was Stephanie, a beautiful brown-haired girl with amazing lips, who could torment any boy in the whole school when she spoke French and her lips made the most fabulous kissing motions.

Angela, too, could form the French words with a superb shape of her broad lips. Her hair was much darker than Stephanie's, thick and rich. She often wore flannel shirts over thermal weave shirts, with basic denim below. Her dark skin and dreadlocks guaranteed she was the topic of many boys' dreams.

And there was Crystal, a blond-haired girl who demanded the attention of many. Her style was similar to Angela's, but Crystal had a fresh-off-the-farm look. A country girl like that probably had every boy in the school dreaming of becoming an agricultural specialist.

Djonny had no intention or inclination to trade in his black leather boots for stable muckers. Though he would admit all of the girls in French class were beautiful, he could think only of the girl who wasn't there.

He woke from his reverie to find all female eyes on him. He had entered the room and forgotten to sit down, standing at the head of the class where the teacher would often lecture. In the absence of the routine teacher, Djonny's classmates stared at him, waiting, expecting something. He doubted he could conduct a whole class, considering his present vocabulary in French was limited only to love songs—and judging from the way the girls were looking at him, that might have led to places he wasn't prepared to go.

He couldn't speak. He could only play music, and though most of the time that fact was liberating, now it felt limiting. A country song came to mind, and Djonny began playing that, timidly, quietly.

To his surprise, Crystal said two words—"Boot scoot"—and she and the rest of the class surged forward and began line dancing. There wasn't a one of them who didn't know the steps. For a moment, Djonny thought he might be more comfortable with those French phrases he was avoiding. Then Crystal called him up.

"Hey, Djonny! Why aren't you dancing?"

Rather than interrupting the song and their collective fun, he just shrugged his shoulders and turned up the volume.

"Come on," she said, "I'll show you how."

Other girls beckoned him, and he could see no good reason to turn down that sort of peer pressure, so he got right in the middle of them.

He missed quite a few of the steps and felt awkward when he caught sight of the rest of them dancing so well, but he started to catch the rhythm of the moves and was slapping boots in no time. His music, their instruction; it was a whole class effort. No one seemed too concerned that the teacher was missing in action, so when the country song ended, Djonny slid right into an alternative song.

A few of the girls sat down, claiming they needed a rest, but the majority of them stayed on the teacher's raised platform to dance. Especially excited about this song was Stephanie, who claimed it was her favorite. Djonny stayed and pretended to dance, mimicking Stephanie's movements. This type of dancing was far less structured than the line dancing, and it didn't seem to matter how Djonny moved.

"You're doing great," Stephanie told him.

How does she know what I'm thinking? he thought.

Pondering over her apparent telepathy, Djonny began to feel a different emotion in his motions. The mood caught him and propelled him to stirring gyrations that excluded rather than included. He was dancing by himself, and the action didn't seem so far different from the line dancing—at least not in his mind.

Alicia, another student, came up to him and whispered a request into his ear. He nodded. He was in a groove now, and the next song blended smoothly in with the last.

The new song was actually old—'80s music, made in the '90s and remade in the '00s. It was a rap song, and the students were mostly loving it. Almost all of them were up on the dance floor now, with only a few sitting it out. Those hopping around the improvised dance floor were squealing at all the fun they were having with the bassline beat. The poetry was decent, Djonny thought. The song was probably one his friend Beto would love, and Djonny wished Beto could be there to knock the dance floor out cold. His moves would have made the girls swoon like dazed groupies.

Djonny saw Kay in the crowd of dancers—the crazy girl who had started his trouble that day. He didn't even know she was in his class, but he was glad to see she was on the other side of the room. There, too, was Pam. Djonny had no idea she liked the style of music he was playing, but there she was, dancing with the rest of them. It occurred to him that he had no idea *she* had ever been in his French class, either.

Pam was an interesting one. She always seemed so depressed. He remembered her voicing her dislike of Roxie and his own agreement at the time. He felt he might grow to dislike Pam based on that minor moment in time. Then he remembered his policy of being too lazy to hold a grudge, and he decided to cue up a goth rock song for Pam.

The song he chose blended nicely with the previous one, making him feel like a skilled deejay. Pam screamed in a pitch much higher than her usual voice when she heard the song, and for the first time, she actually looked happy.

After Pam's song, Djonny played a pop number for Marla, followed by a classic dance song for Misty. Gina asked for a hardcore song, and her Hawaiian friend Bonnie requested Israel Kamakawiwo'ole, who Djonny was surprised to discover in his library. While the gentle sounds of ukulele played, most of the girls took a water break. A few stayed to attempt a hula dance, which they started to accomplish after a short while of instructing and correcting one another. When the sweet island sounds ended, there was an uproar for more.

More music. Infinite music.

"Come on, Djonny," Crystal said, "gimme another country song."

"Another rocker!" said Susan.

"Another goth rocker," Pam argued, her voice gloomy again.

"Hey, I didn't get one yet," Angela protested.

"That's right," Djonny said. "No requests . . . from Angie."

"Angela," she corrected him.

"Well, what does Angela enjoy?"

"Hip-hop," Gina guessed.

But Angela shook her head and pulled a sour face. "Don't stereotype me."

"Country?" Crystal guessed hopefully.

Angela laughed sweetly. "Nope."

"Australian death metal?"

"No."

"Swedish polka?"

"No way."

"Alternative country?" Crystal guessed again.

"You mean like Slim Cessna?" Angela asked.

"Right."

"Not today."

"What is it?" Djonny asked in his sing-song voice. "We've guessed almost everything."

Angela looked around the room, perhaps surprised no one knew her well enough to know what kind of music she liked, and perhaps expecting more guesses. She closed her eyes for her personal revelation. "Industrial."

"Oh," Crystal said, "like electronica and techno?"

"Yeah," Angela said, and expounded: "But more with, like, movie sound bites and metallic beats made by hammers on anvils."

Getting a sudden notion, Djonny went to the wall behind the teacher's podium and selected a cable from the sound system. Designed for teachers to amplify their voices and save their vocal cords, the system had everything Djonny needed except for the delivery device. He remembered the extra player he had in his pocket and sent blessings toward the source of that acquisition.

Who was that, again? Right. As if I could forget her.

He laughed at his personal joke, quickly found a song for Angela called "Glass Houses," cued it up, and watched as all the girls began dancing again.

Time, Djonny decided, *to exit.*

He left the sound system playing on a random queue and made his way quietly out the door.

18. The Rich Man Keeps What the Poor Man Throws Away

"Students, between-class flossing will get that embarrassing husk out of your teeth. Bruce Wingate, stop playing your guitar in the chemistry hallway, you're causing a traffic jam. Paul Richard, you're talking too fast, we can't understand a word you're saying. Dave Scott is drumming on level three, and his arms are moving so fast you can't even see them. One more thing to remember, students: Please stop asking the philosophy teacher unanswerable questions. And don't Google it, either. We only have a finite amount of infonet out there, you know."

Ayden found Djonny first. He told him how sorry he was that he couldn't make it to their previously set meeting, but his leg was bothering him, and he'd gone to get first aid for the wound.

"Sarcastic, are we?" Djonny said flatly.

"No. I just have this strange aversion to pain. Can you believe that?"

"You don't mind giving it. Taking it was never your style."

"Hey, not quite fair, is it? I mean, where are *you* hurt?"

"Nowhere you can see . . ."

"So where, then?"

Roxie approached and looked at them expectantly. Djonny tried to guess what she was after, ready to ignore the minor argument with Ayden.

"Pleased to meet you, ma'am," Djonny said.

Roxie grabbed Djonny and Ayden by the arms and pointed down the hall with her lips. Stalker Mick stared purposefully in their direction. She briskly ushered the two boys away.

"Boy, that guy is so creepy," Djonny said.

They pushed against the current of bodies pressing down the halls and found the same restroom as before. Roxie scouted it and found it empty. Djonny gave the okay sign to the nearest security camera, and the three went inside.

"I brought a really good pen, give me space," Ayden said. His voice echoed in the acoustic space on the tile walls.

Roxie obliged, and Ayden went to work on Djonny. His first stroke was swift and angry. His stance was horselike and forced.

"Do you need a laxative?" Djonny asked.

"I have to get in the mood," Ayden said.

"You have to be in the mood for a laxative?" Roxie said.

"Nooo!" Ayden snapped. "I have to be in the right frame of mind to put graffiti on someone. And I don't need a laxative. Just sit still and let me make you a piece of art."

"Most art *is* still," Djonny noted, tensing himself to avoid wiggling.

"Right," Ayden said as he slashed with the paint pen, drawing across one of the speakers in Djonny's jacket. Djonny played the next thing in line to check that the speaker still worked.

"And my art is mine," Djonny said. "Don't take it from me."

Ayden took careful aim and made seven more marks in quick succession, followed by half a dozen more. He approached like a fencing pro, then backed away to admire the stabs he had made. Every second brought him—them—closer to the masterpiece. At one point, he admired his work long enough to make them wonder if he was finished.

"That looks really good," Roxie told him.

"Shush," Ayden said as he finished one crazy gang sign and went to work on another. He was finding his groove and making the art as real as possible. It was no overstated modern art, but to the uninitiated eye, it would certainly appear that way.

Except for the small clown face he drew at the bottom of Djonny's jacket, everything was sloppy, jagged lettering, rendering Djonny a walking graffiti billboard. Ayden even told him so. "If you don't wash it off soon, it will become permanent."

"I thought it was all . . . permanent," Djonny said with a quizzical expression.

Ayden shook his head. "No, it shouldn't be. I mean, a leather jacket should resist the paint, right? You could probably wash it off with some plain soap and water and cover any misses with shoe polish, but the longer it stays on, the more it will soak into cracks and pores."

"Pores," Djonny echoed.

"Right," said Roxie. "I know what he means. And I know what you mean too, Djonny. I thought Mick's paint pen was permanent too. Anyway, school's almost over. Then you can go home and wash it off."

"I could," Djonny said, "but now that it's a piece of art . . ."

"It does look pretty good," Roxie said.

"Thanks," Ayden said, admiring his work.

Djonny pointed to a white smudge on one of his wrists. "What's this?"

"Sorry. I guess I got carried away."

"Here," Roxie offered, pulling a lacey handkerchief out of her purse and handing it to Djonny. She snatched it out of his hands before he could get a grip on it, stepped to one of the sinks on the wall, wet it down, and handed it back.

Djonny rubbed the smudge so vigorously his skin turned red.

"Not so hard," Roxie said.

"I love this lace," Djonny said.

Ayden pointed at the handkerchief. "I wonder if that'll come clean."

Djonny laughed through his threads. "White on white . . . shouldn't matter."

"You can keep it anyway," Roxie told him.

It was Ayden's turn to laugh. "Now you made his day. He'll cherish that lace forever."

"And never let it go," Djonny added with a wink and a smile.

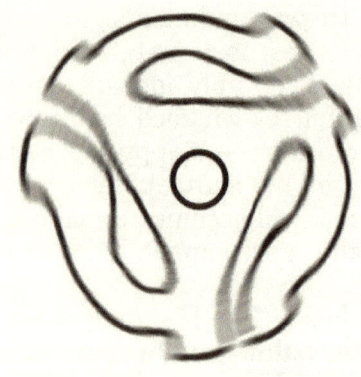

19. Change Your Name to Fit the Band

"As the day draws to a close, remember to keep your pencils sharp, your mind's even sharper, and if you're going to sneeze in an elbow, make it someone else's elbow. You don't want that junk on you."

Mister Lyster taught science. He was possibly the most mysterious teacher ever, with his tasteless style in clothing leaning toward the acrylic blends and a propensity for decorating his classroom with pyramids.

Lyster's teaching style was more distant than that of the others. Many times, his students were taught more by the television than by him. Sometimes, he would only leave instructions to be followed on the whiteboard. There, on the board, a giant red arrow stood out boldly against the white background. It pointed up to one of the windows. In the corner of the window was a spider's web. In the web was a fat and healthy spider, which looked even larger because of its long, spindly legs. Inside the arrow on the whiteboard were the words: *Check that out!*

The instructions on the whiteboard had nothing to do with the spider. They were instead instructions to each student to select a formaldehyde jar from the shelves and begin dissecting whatever was contained in the jar. Scientific principles were to be used to find all the attributes of the pickled specimen, and the answers were due at the end of class.

There was a fair amount of grumbling at this assignment as the students rolled into the classroom and saw their polyester-wearing teacher slumped comfortably in his padded chair as if he were asleep. He clutched a miniature replica of the Great Pyramid of Giza in his sleeping hands.

Though some complained, a few students in the class joyfully accepted the challenge. Hiro began testing his scalpel skills against Isaiah Johnson's right away. Isaiah tested back, giving Hiro the game-face of a pro. Noah Johnson, however, took his time selecting a specimen, staring long and hard at each jar with only one eye—as if one eye was good, the other bad.

Djonny managed to find something unidentifiable. He gripped the jar suspiciously and found his usual chair. The jar made a loud pop when he opened it. He plopped the contents into a metal tray. After selecting a scalpel, he cut into the strange, grey form. He sliced with one hand and took notes with the other.

Able to distract his students even while sleeping, Mister Lyster began to snore. His limp form did not move, but the sound was loud enough to make Djonny imagine a revving engine.

"With that much torque," Djonny told the girl next to him, "the frame should twist."

A girl named Joan sat to Djonny's left. She nodded. "I expect him to jump out of his seat any minute." Joan was carving slowly and delicately on a squid. The squid had retained its original hues, despite being preserved in formaldehyde.

"Yours is so much more colorful than mine," Djonny told her. "I wonder why."

She studied his dissection project for a solid minute, then said, "I don't even know *what* that is."

Djonny poked at the form in the tray. He turned it over with a less-than-gentle prod. It appeared to have a tail that had been smashed to its body from being stuffed in the jar. Djonny peeled the tail away to discover it had been covering one of the creature's eyes. The thing seemed to be looking at him—gazing intently with that single staring eye.

Djonny tried in vain to stick the tail back over the eye, but the beast's hairless flesh was too slick.

Without seeing the motion or hearing movement, Djonny sensed a presence near him. It was Mister Lyster, leaning over the table and staring down at the grey shape in the tray.

It didn't startle Djonny, but Joan jumped out of her boondockers. She left her leather boots on the floor, snatched up her trayful of squid, and plodded in stockings to a table far from Mister Lyster. Once positioned, she glared at Lyster suspiciously.

"I have that effect on some," Lyster said. "What is it you're working on, Mister DeSoto?"

"Identification."

"Very good. Any conclusions?" Lyster put his hands behind his back, leaning in closer to the grey lump in Djonny's tray.

"Only that I wish it would stop looking at me," Djonny said.

Mister Lyster coughed. "It's not looking at you, it's looking at me."

"Really? What makes you say that?"

"Am I not the one who put it in its jar?"

"Well, if you did that . . . then you should know what it is."

Lyster stood up straight. He scratched old man fingernails against his polyester shirt. The sound was disturbing. It sounded like something was trying to get out of his shirt. "I can't remember," he said.

"How long has it been?" Djonny's eyes looked amazed, but his voice remained level.

Lyster didn't answer; a visitor was poking his head in the classroom door.

Djonny recognized the tall man's greying temples, and the lab coat and business attire underneath. It was Doctor Virgil Connor. Mister Lyster went dutifully to the door to greet his visitor.

"Come in, come in, my friend," said Lyster.

Virgil held a clear plastic bin. There was a black lid covering the bin, but everyone could see what was inside. It was stuffed from bottom to top with tree frogs.

"These have died," Virgil told Lyster. He spoke quietly, but everyone in the room heard him. "I thought you could use them in your class."

"We can, thanks. Do you want to stay? Or do you need to get back to your store?"

Virgil considered the offer. "What are you doing today?"

"Clearing the shelves."

"Well, then, I'm right on time!" Virgil handed Lyster the bin of tree frogs. As he did this, Djonny spied movement inside of it.

"They're alive!" Djonny exclaimed, not realizing he was shouting. He quickly adjusted the volume on his device. "Sorry. I didn't know I was so loud. I thought I saw . . . one of them moved!"

"That was melodic," Virgil said, approaching Djonny. "You look familiar."

Djonny laughed behind his threads. "Everyone knows me." He held his arms out to better display his jacket and its art.

Virgil's head shook, and his brow creased. "What does that mean?"

"Don't worry. Never mind." Djonny waved a hand dismissively. "Better if you tell me . . . what do you think *that* is?" He stared down at the strange grey thing in his tray. It lay like a solid lump of alien flesh. It had limbs, but they were so smashed into the greater mass that it was difficult to count them or to discern arms from legs.

Obviously prepared, Virgil snapped a pair of latex gloves out of his coat pocket. He stretched them, put them on his hands, and picked up a scalpel from the table. He held the thing in the pan with one hand and sawed into it with the scalpel. His focus was on the creature's visible eye, but he made such a wild path to get to it that the grey lump was becoming even more unrecognizable.

"Finally," Virgil said as something came free from the creature. He grabbed hold of the severed item, but it was so wet that it squirted like a watermelon seed and disappeared among the students' legs.

Hiro leapt over the projectile. "*Ya-daa*! What was that!?"

"The beginning of a horror movie," Djonny said.

"Actually," Virgil corrected, "it was a pineal evocator. See if you can find it."

"If you know the parts," Djonny said, "then you must know the whole."

Virgil stared down at the grey thing and shook his head sadly. "Sorry. I don't know. I have some guesses, but it could be many things. If we had some kind of scanner, we could get a closer idea."

"This *is* the science lab," Mister Lyster said as he stashed the bin of frogs behind his desk. "We have a scanner. But my pride and joy died last week."

"He means his computer," a student named Jack said.

"Oo, I have a computer that can sit up and beg," said Djonny. "I could . . . run to get it."

"Sure," Lyster said, stepping back out of Djonny's way.

Djonny didn't wait for further debate. He ran out to the hall and turned in the direction of the Computer Lab. He sprinted along a hall lined with lockers and took a stairway down to the next floor. He sprinted again but slowed before he could get going very far. A group of boys occupied one of the short halls to his left. They were engaged in what looked like an all-out battle.

It was the cowboys against the hardcore boys. There were boots of all kinds. Fists flew in every direction. There were arms flinging fists and boots kicking boots. There was a cowboy standing on top of the face of one of the hardcore boys, digging his boots in.

Mysteriously, the boy had a smile on his squashed face.

"Is everything cool?" Djonny asked curiously.

The boy on the floor answered with a laugh. One of his friends tackled the cowboy, and he jumped to his feet. "Everything's all riot here," he said and jumped into the fray.

It didn't look all right. There were at least two boys with bloody noses, and one of the hardcore boys was holding his teeth in his hand. He made a fist around the teeth and punched someone with it.

Djonny walked away slowly, eyes glued to the ensuing fight.

While he watched, a cowboy and a hardcore boy hit each other in the eye at the same time. Both went down as the fight continued around them.

Shrugging his shoulders, Djonny continued down the hall. He couldn't figure out some people's pastimes.

He found the Computer Lab empty, which was odd, though not entirely rare. He grabbed up the device he'd created earlier in the day and went back down the hall. He jogged the best he could with the electronics cradled in his arms, trying not to drop the newly-born advanced calculator.

As he passed the short hall where the fight had been, he saw the hall completely deserted.

Strange things . . . are happening here . . . all around me, surrounding me.

He met Roxie coming down the hall from one of the classrooms.

"Hey," she said. She smiled, and he smiled with her.

He set the computer on the hallway floor. "Hey," he said.

"You're funny."

"Sometimes. They're going to miss you . . ." Djonny pointed at the classroom behind her.

"No, the teacher is so caught up in what's on the board, he doesn't know what happens behind him." She dropped her smile and looked concerned. "Are you doing okay? You look like you lost a contest or something."

"I don't know. Some people are missing."

"Well, where did you leave them?"

"Right where they were before."

"Huh," Roxie said and scrunched her face in thought. "You know, people go where they're gonna go. They turn up later. Anyway, I wanted to ask you what your last class is."

"Fax." Although he meant F.A.C.S., he figured she would understand.

"Do you mind if I drop in? I have free time for my last class. I can go to any one I want."

"Please, please, please do," he said. And then, because it felt right, he bowed at the end of the musical plea.

"Great! See you there."

Roxie skipped back into the classroom; her teacher hadn't noticed a thing.

Djonny scooped up his electronics and finished the trip back to science class. Fully expecting the class to be empty of occupants when he opened the door, he was pleasantly surprised to see everyone there. Virgil was again poking with a scalpel at the grey lump. Mister Lyster had the scanner next to the tray, ready to be connected to an electronic brain. That was what Djonny intended to provide. He set up his computer and plugged in the scanner.

After typing a few commands, he shooed Virgil away. He pulled the scanner over the strange thing and focused its aperture. When he had what he thought was a decent shot, he threw his device into overdrive. Images flashed on the computer screen at about seven per second. It was going through all of the known or accessible images to find any that had similar qualities.

As the images flashed across the screen, some of the students gathered around. Djonny thought he saw the base image change from the grey lump to a diaphanous tadpole to a bioluminescent cavefish and back. He blinked and rubbed his eyes.

Virgil put a hand on Djonny's shoulder. "You're going to get over it. You're going to be okay. You're going to die like one of my tree frogs."

Djonny stared at the old man suspiciously out of the corner of his eye, saying nothing about his contrary statement.

At the three-minute mark, the program ended, and a bell sounded from the computer. Virgil and Djonny shifted their attention. It had selected one million pictures with similar qualities. Knowing this was too many, Djonny refined the search. Thirty seconds later, he had the results.

"Really," Virgil said, reading the results. He looked to the screen and back at the form in the tray. "I guess it could be."

"I've never heard of one of those," said Noah from behind Djonny.

"I've heard of them," Djonny said. "But I never imagined . . . all the eyes."

"We used to have one in a tank on our patio," Hiro said.

For a moment, everyone stared at Hiro as if he had a foul stench about him. He got several moans for this untimely revelation.

Kevin slugged him in the shoulder playfully. "Why didn't you say so?"

"I wasn't sure, since it's so mashed up," Hiro said, ducking away as some of the students rubbed their knuckles on his head.

"Children, children," said Mister Lyster, trying to calm the students.

Virgil said, "A Japanese tiger lobster should be mounted as a trophy, not dissected in a science class."

Djonny nodded. "Did anyone manage to find . . . its third eye?"

20. Staring Down the Grooves of a 45

"Whoever is dropping their vegetables down the heater vent in the lunch room, the custodians would like to warn you that your DNA was found in that pile of green beans last week, and the asparagus this week had your teeth marks in it, so it won't be long before your dentist and your ancestors identify you. By the way, the lunch ladies say they have good news and bad news, but you'll have to decide for yourself: They've run out of mystery meat, so tomorrow's lunch will be all vegetables."

Sick Mick had been following Djonny around all day. Djonny didn't notice much. He was so distracted, in fact, that he even turned a corner quickly and pounded right into the resident psycho.

Mick acted alarmed and shocked. He flailed his arms in the air as if set off balance (though everyone nearby saw that his feet didn't move at all). He blinked and spat a couple of times to show everyone something had happened to him—and probably to get more attention.

"Why don't you watch where I'm going?" Sick Mick snapped.

Pausing only slightly to catch his balance, Djonny tried to hide his fear. "We meet again . . . strangers . . . enemies and friends."

"Not friends," Mick argued. "Never friends."

"If you're friendly, everyone is your friend."

"I don't make it a habit of making friends."

"Habit-forming things should be avoided. Thinking . . . is a bad habit everyone should quit."

Mick paused, baffled. He wasn't quite sure what was going on with this confrontation. It was not going at all the same way any other confrontation he'd ever had before. Mick had always struck enough fear into his enemies that they cowered before him. This one was being far too playful. Feeling compelled, Mick optioned for the kill.

"I'm not impressed with your stupid songs," Mick said. "No matter what you play, I won't dance. No matter what you play, I'm still fighting you after school."

Djonny shook his head. "Everybody has a song inside. Some just take longer to find one they like."

"You don't know me. I don't care."

"Kay . . . likes popular music."

"You leave her out of this! How do you know about that,

anyway?"

"She was in my . . . French class . . . on the dance floor with all the other Betties. Dancing to the music . . . that moved her body."

Mick grew angrier. He squinted his eyes as if to shut out the fires of Hades. His lips reared back, revealing his teeth. His breathing became hot and ragged.

Djonny playfully hoped he hadn't made things worse, still knowing that Kay was the reason this whole thing got started. She and her daring friends were the reason Mick aimed the crazy toward him.

"Why are you paying attention to my girl?!" Mick shouted.

"I'm not! I'm the deejay. I help them find . . . the song that makes them want to dance . . . the beat . . . the dance floor."

"You're a stalker! You're stalking my girlfriend."

As Mick's voice grew louder, a crowd began to gather around, their innate morbid curiosity compelling them to watch.

The long-haired rockers were there first, grinning like hounds on the scent. Djonny could see them directly behind Mick. To the left of the rockers was Harold, munching on a hot dog, his fingers yellowed with mustard. The vending machines stood in the background. The soda hologram had turned to a display of Djonny and Mick facing each other. Djonny saw Roxie and Ayden down the hall. The sight of Roxie was encouraging.

Realizing it was time to change his tactic, Djonny said, "Who's been following me around all day?"

"You stay away from my girlfriend!" Mick screamed.

"Didn't I see you this morning?"

"You can't turn this around on me!"

Djonny repeated Mick's words, mimicking his voice perfectly. "You're a stalker!"

"Now you've crossed the line, punk. I never gave you permission to record my voice. I'll sue you into the ground."

"Oh, I see, you know the law. You have a lawyer . . ."

"I never said that!"

"You said your middle name is Sue . . ."

"Let's just fight now," Mick said, his frustration peaking. "Why wait?" He threw his arms up, slapped them at his thighs, and took a step closer. Though the gesture was too silly to be threatening, it did draw a crowd. The number of spectators doubled instantly. The doubling set Djonny's nerves, but it only encouraged Mick to further his antics.

"I don't play music, but I do have a forty-five," Mick said, sounding oddly poetic. He pulled a handgun from under his jacket and aimed it at Djonny's head. Mick opened his mouth as if he was going to say something, but before he could, a loud voice sounded from the crowd.

It was a girl's voice, but Djonny wasn't quite sure whose. "Don't shoot him, he's a Beatle!"

Everyone looked around, trying to find the source of the voice, but no one was able to pinpoint it. The mysterious girl said no more. Mick took on a look of cold determination. His squinty eyes twitched, making him appear all the crazier.

An idea caught hold of Djonny's brain. He thumbed quickly and discreetly through his media utility device while keeping his eyes on Mick. Djonny's device displayed what he wanted to know: There were many similar devices with speakers nearby.

Djonny tapped all of the devices he could and made them simultaneously play the same song at the highest volume. Adrenalin O.D.'s "Sleep" blew out a few of the speakers, but there were enough left that the sound bombarded Mick from all sides. He put his hands up to his ears to shut out the sound but couldn't block it out for the gun in his hand.

Donny manipulated the song, making it distort and throb, alternating through louder vocals, louder guitars, and louder drums. Mick's expression transformed from confused to frightened. He threw the gun to the floor and clapped both hands to his ears. His eyes circled his slits, bulging the eyelids as they oscillated.

The long-haired rockers were having a thrash-fest behind Mick. Their hair whipped around like happy, wagging dog tails. Most of the other students started getting into the song as well.

The song ended sooner than Djonny wanted, so he brought up "Schizophrenia" by Descendents. That did it. There was enough feedback and distortion in that song to make Mick as insane as he wanted everyone to believe he was. His hands clamped down on his head, and his face began to redden.

Through the cacophony, there came a voice from the crowd. "Excuse me, sorry," said Mister Morgen. He held a long white cane with a red tip, tapping it against the floor and against the students' shins as he pushed his way through the crowd. "Pardon me. Blind man coming through. Wow, it seems there are more students every year!"

Mister Morgen did his slow tap strut and brushed past Mick,

exiting quietly out the other side of the gathered crowd. "Excuse me . . . excuse me," he said as he went, making his entrance and departure a bit surreal.

When Djonny looked back, Mick was still frozen in the haunted stance. Djonny turned off the music. As he looked at his device, he also looked at the floor. The gun was gone.

Mister Morgen?

Mick took into account the lack of handgun in his own hand and saw nothing on the floor, but he didn't know what to do about it.

Djonny held his arms out steady, a submissive offering to Mick's weaponless hands. "By the way," he said, "my middle name is. . . gang sign."

Mick finally noticed the art all over Djonny's jacket. Some of it was familiar to him. His mouth fell open as his eyes wandered across the jacket, catching sight of too many frightening things.

"Where did you—? There's no one who wants that much damage."

"I suck damage like vampires suck blood," Djonny said.

"You have business with the clowns. Clowns give me the heebie-jeebies."

Djonny was stunned. Here was the school psycho, a guy who brought fear on everyone, confessing his fear of clowns. Djonny had never understood the fear. Clowns were silly, no matter how you dressed them up. To Djonny, being afraid of clowns was like being afraid of kittens, or marshmallows, or pimples.

". . . or wheelchairs, or old ladies in pink pajamas, or those comic characters on cereal boxes, or stretch limo hummers . . ." Djonny stopped when he caught himself thinking out loud, hoping no one understood what he was saying. He lifted his thumb.

Mick just nodded and said nothing, as if agreeing with Djonny's thoughts. Djonny knew it wasn't safe, or even polite, to make assumptions. He changed the subject. "Hey listen. If you see Kay . . ."

"What about her?" Mick said, offended again. He moved to shove Djonny but backed off when he looked at the symbols on his jacket again.

"She likes pop music," Djonny said. "She likes to dance. Show her a good time. Give her romance."

Mick couldn't decide if he should finish his business with Djonny or cut and run. It was risky either way. The kid was obviously unstable—anyone who could gather that many gang signs in one day was definitely insane—and Mick, believing himself to be rather sane, did not want the insanity to rub off on him in a fight.

Still, Mick knew that if the crowd saw him leave, they would all think him weak. And if that happened, he would no longer rule the hallways. His territory would diminish; his influence would dry up. He would no longer be the school genius. Teachers would start giving him homework again. And worst of all, they might not let him keep his Bouga toad in his locker. Now that was too much!

Once again, Mick approached Djonny with the flapping of his arms. "I ain't afraid of you," he hissed. "You're so scrawny and weak!" He flapped his arms again, slapping them down against his thighs.

Djonny stood still. Then he curled his arms up by his head and flexed, showing how his biceps bulged inside the jacket. "Genetic weakness . . . is harder to see."

"What's that supposed to mean?" Mick growled, tilting his head to one side, his squinty eyes as unfathomable as ever. He was trying to be scary, but it was apparent that he was the one who was scared.

"It means," Djonny said, "that to know scrawny takes more time than . . . ten rounds, twelve rounds, thirteen rounds. How many rounds do you want?"

A boy near the rockers said, "Oo, Djonny's gonna hurt that little boy Mick."

Mick's head came up straight and his eyes widened. He looked around, a rabbit among foxes. Then he singled someone out from the crowd. "You! I saw you laugh at me! I'm going to fight you after I fight him!"

Harold was standing next to the student Mick had called out. He put on a face. There was a small dab of mustard at the corner of his lips. "No you won't," Harold said softly.

Djonny laughed. "You see, he's the fist for the pacifist."

Mick knew he was losing it. Losing control was an uncomfortable thing. Losing power was like being undressed in public.

Seeing Mick's nerves jumping and his brain collapsing, Djonny tried to help. "You don't even have to fight me. I told you to romance your woman. If you do that . . . she probably won't be kissing other people . . . though a lot of it had to do with her friends daring her. So anyway, what's it going to be? Pay attention to what matters, or pay attention to me?"

Mick thought about it for only a second. "Kay."

"Yes, you see Kay . . . you suck . . . face."

Something happened then that caused the gathered crowd to gasp: Mick laughed. No one had ever heard him laugh before. It was an awkward sound, but a laugh all the same. Djonny had made Sick Mick laugh.

The crowd held its breath to see what would happen next. Would these two become friends? Would Mick flap his arms again like an offended turkey? Would Djonny flex again or play a full song instead of only brief bursts? Would Harold protect them all from a beating? Would anyone fight today?

Mick pulled himself together. He wasn't about to give the crowd another laugh. Even though it felt good to laugh, he knew they wouldn't let him be a tough guy among them if he giggled about everything. Next, he'd be following Jill Renee around, begging her for more jokes.

Djonny had similar thoughts. If he could get Kay to become one of Jill Renee's followers, Djonny thought, Mick would probably follow her as well. And If Mick followed the comic queen around, he would definitely start laughing more.

Almost as if on cue, Jill Renee and her followers came through the circle, laughing boisterously at one of her latest word-spins, oblivious to the tension in the hallway.

Mick took advantage of the interruption to fuel his escape. "I'm going to suck face," he said, as if it had been his idea all along. He pushed his way out of the circle.

Everyone watched in amazement at the psycho boy's departure.

"Hey, Mister Music," Jill Renee called out to Djonny. "Will you play me another funny?"

"How do you get stains out of leather?" Djonny replied.

"I don't know. How?"

Djonny shrugged. "Buck knife. Lead pipe. Sand blast. Wet lace."

The confusion was evident on Jill Renee's face as she giggled politely and walked away.

21. If You're Foxy, I'm Comin' to Get Ya

"Any resemblance to real news is a complete coincidence . . ." The intercom clicked and buzzed, sounding ominous without human hands to manipulate it or a human voice to give it purpose.

All the students were standing around their cooking stations, waiting to see what the recipe of the day would be. It was not uncommon for someone to try to sneak a text message to their friends by holding their cell phone beyond the sight of the teacher, somewhere below the counter and stove heights and in the vicinity of the student's crotch. This was the worst thing anyone could do in Miss Orleans' class, though, she being a highly vocal person and not intimidated at all by her students.

"Hey!" Miss Orleans yelled playfully. "No *texterbating* in my classroom!"

Sadly, it was Beto who was caught in the act. He didn't know what to do about his indiscretion, or being caught at it, so he threw his phone in the nearest oven and slammed the door. Everyone in the class, including Miss Orleans, burst out laughing at this show of nervousness.

"What?" Beto said as if nothing whatsoever had happened. His face was reddening in spite of his false show of calmness.

"Dazzle them with dance," Djonny advised, playing a quiet tune in the funk vein, and Beto took the advice.

Beto did a spin move that took him down to the floor and, still spinning, he came up again. With a series of sidesteps, he stood in the middle of the room and held his arms out, his head down, his feet slightly apart. From there, he dropped down into the splits and came up smiling and doing a can-can.

Some of the girls laughed, and Beto ate up the love. He paused, did a brief jig, and slid into a hip-slide-arm-tug that took him down the aisle. His shoes made a squeak on the linoleum as he spun around and went back the other way with a cross-armed flutter step many of the girls in the class knew. They joined him and began moving the same way. It was very much like the line dance Djonny had participated in earlier.

Next to Djonny, at his cooking station, was Roxie. Like Djonny, she did not join in the dance that was taking Beto and his bevy out the classroom door.

Djonny and Roxie looked at each other as the last of the girls went out the door. Djonny suggested, "Let's watch the parade," so they both ran for the door and watched as Beto and the girls continued their dance routine through the hall.

For a moment, it looked as if they were going to go around the whole school doing their dance, entertaining the beleaguered class-bound students who were all ready for school to be over.

"Now that's . . . community service," Djonny said.

Roxie agreed, too busy watching and enjoying the show to get his whole meaning.

Turning back, they realized they were alone in the room. Miss Orleans had left a recipe on her display screen and had gone somewhere. The display was a recipe for pumpkin pie, and the title scrolled and flashed at the top.

"Mmm," said Roxie. "I love pumpkin pie. Shall we make some?"

Djonny nodded solemnly. "Absolutely . . . sounds divine."

They began collecting ingredients. Miss Orleans had a can pyramid of pureed pumpkin on her desk. They took one, got out the mixing bowls and the measuring cups and spoons, and began dealing out the proper amounts.

"Let's see," said Roxie. "It says we need four eggs. Those must be in the fridge. I'll get them."

While she was away in the walk-in refrigerator, Djonny pulled Beto's phone from the oven where he'd deposited it. There was an alphanumeric message displayed on the screen from someone by the curious name of Alicesteria: *o left 2 lose*

Djonny scrolled through the rest of the message history.

Beto: *What about your friends, me, Your pet boa*

Alicesteria: *Not my family*

Beto: *Lots 2 lose + U wd be lost 2 us*

Alicesteria: *Dred a day w/ dad him or me*

Beto: *How can I convice U?*

The conversation ended there. Djonny knew nothing about this girl, but his emotions were triggered by her desperate letters. He wanted to help her. He composed the reply: *Are you still there? This is Djonny, not Beto.*

Alicesteria: *Hi DJ What do u want?*

Beto: *I'm on Beto's phone. I was just wondering if everything is okay. It says you have a pet boa. Could I see it sometime? I have a pet black widow.*

Alicesteria: *Yr not DJ Yr Beto Stop trying*

Beto: *No seriously, I'm Djonny. Tell me your number and I'll call you from my MUD.*

Alicesteria's number came up on the screen at the same time Roxie returned with the eggs. Djonny laid Beto's phone on the counter. "Check this out," he said.

Roxie set the eggs down and read the messages on Beto's phone. "Hmm," Roxie said, "sounds troubled. Maybe I should talk to her. You *guys* are usually less than subtle. You know what I mean?"

Djonny nodded as he composed a text to Alicesteria: *See here. And see, hear. (Audio file attached.)*

There was a pause long enough for the girl to listen to the short piece of cheer Djonny had sent her. It was a happy tune by the Blackwater Fever called "Breakdown."

Roxie began tapping rapidly with her thumbs on Beto's phone. Then she started laughing.

"What is it?" Djonny asked.

"Nothing. Oh, you didn't," she said, still typing.

"Nothing? How can it be nothing?"

"You gave her the blues?"

"Yeah, of course. A blues song always has the power to cheer me up."

"This is exactly what I was saying. You boys have no tact. No subtlety. No sympathy."

Roxie set Beto's phone back down on the counter next to the eggs. "The girl's going to be alright," she said. "I got it all straightened out."

"What did you say?"

"Never mind. Look, here's your proof." She held up Beto's phone. The message from Alicesteria read: *Thanx Roxie. I'll be alright now. C U soon.*

"Wow," Djonny said, sincerity evident on his face. "How do you do it? You even got her . . . to use punctuation. She doesn't spell well. But I mean, you even got her . . . to use punctuation!"

Roxie took the compliment well. She grinned. "Let me just say that we girls know each other better than any boy ever will."

"That is a shame," Djonny said, bumping her playfully with his hip.

"Shall we make that pie now?"

"I *am* hungry."

"It's amazing that guys feel anything."

"I feel concern for the girl," he said, pointing at Beto's phone, then at his stomach. "And hunger."

They laughed. It felt good to laugh together.

Djonny took another look at the recipe. Without another word about Alicesteria, he turned the oven on, opened the door, and searched the inside. "Just making sure . . . no more cell phones."

Roxie laughed and told him to get a mixing bowl from the cupboard while she sent the can of puree through the can opener. It wasn't long before they were pouring pumpkin pie mix into the pie crust and attempting to carry it to the oven without spilling any of it. With four hands on the pie, it was a task more difficult than a three-legged race, and they managed to spill some on Djonny's boot, the floor, and the oven door. As they spilled, so they giggled, and as they giggled, the pie jiggled. With every laugh and guffaw, it became more and more difficult to keep the pie mixture steady.

"We need to go steady," Roxie said through her laughter.

The majority of the pie arrived on the oven rack and intact, no thanks to Djonny's nervously shaking hands. Roxie looked at him and saw his face was turning bright red.

"Was it something I said?" she asked, smiling with conspiratorial confidence. She knew exactly what she was doing.

"I don't . . . yes, I do," Djonny said aloud, his face still a red blur of timid, heart-racing teenage confusion. He knew no romance other than that in his imagination.

"Relax," Roxie said. "I meant we need to go steady with the pie."

Djonny shook his head. "I can't have that kind of relationship . . . with pie."

"Don't worry. Now that it's in," she said, closing the oven door gently, "we only have to wait for it to cook. And then our relationship with the pie can be purely—"

"I know what you mean. Not carnal, but . . ."

"Gustatorial?" she said, stepping closer.

Djonny stepped closer himself. "We still need to clean up."

"That jacket looks really tight in the chest."

"I invented it myself. The sound . . . is in the upper region."

He only had to tilt his head down slightly to reach hers.

"It was sweet of you to loan it to me," she breathed on his cheek and in his ear.

Djonny leaned in for the kiss, and just as he leaned, Miss Orleans burst out of the walk-in refrigerator. She mumbled something about diuretics and long hallways, hammers and coffee mugs. Then she rushed out the door and made a quick right turn, not once acknowledging them.

Roxie laughed. "I didn't see her in there, I swear." She gave Djonny a quick peck on the cheek. "You know, you're right. We need to clean up."

"Wow," Djonny said, "it's a good thing . . . the teacher was here. That might've been really embarrassing. I forgot . . ."

"Yeah, well, it's not so bad. What part of this do you want?" She gestured at the mess they'd created. There were measuring cups and spoons, stirring bowls and more spoons, and a host of spices. Djonny chose the dishes. He rinsed them in the sink and then stacked them in the dishwasher while Roxie put away the spices.

"So the jacket really is amazing," she said. "I think you should sell it."

"What do you mean?"

"You know, sell it to a company that can mass produce them and market them."

"Oh. I gotcha. We could sell them to people who . . . really have no voice."

"Sure," she shrugged, "but that's not what I was thinking. Not really. I was thinking of you making your way in life. What are you going to do when you grow up? Are you going to be an inventor?"

"I could, I guess."

"Well, you're not going to be a chef."

"No . . . I'll eat the pie . . . not cook it."

"What, then? An animal trainer?"

"Genetic modification specialist," Djonny said, thinking of Virgil's pet store.

Roxie shook her head thoughtfully. "No, I just can't see you doing that."

"I could invent things. What about different styles of the jacket . . . The Sporto . . . The Collector, with lots of pockets . . . The Bomber . . . The Business Man, a suit jacket . . . The Biker . . . The Ugly Christmas Sweater that plays lots of Christmas music . . ."

"I don't think you'll sell a lot of those. Too seasonal."

He smiled. "But think of how many people . . . do the ugly sweater thing that time of year." His eyebrows danced as he thought about it.

"Okay, you got me there."

"Anyway, enough about me. What about your future?"

She giggled. "I'm going to be a genetic modification technician."

"You're impossible."

"I was only joking. Anyway, my mom wants me to be a

homemaker, and my dad wants me to be a lawyer like him. Why do parents always want their kids to be exactly like them?"

"Desperate for immortality."

"Huh?"

"Immortality," he repeated. "They want to live forever . . . through you."

"Oh, okay, I've heard of that. What is it called?" She thought for a moment. "I remember! It's called 'vicarious immortality.' We learned about it in Psychology."

"Smart and beautiful . . ."

"You won't get any points for lying."

"I mean it."

"Sure," she said, and as she said it, the oven timer announced the pie was ready.

Djonny put on the oven mittens and Roxie opened the oven door. He reached in, removed it carefully, and placed it on the stovetop.

Roxie stuck a toothpick in the center of the pie, pulled it out clean, and pronounced it worthy. "It's done. We'll have to let it cool off a bit, though."

"How about some whipped cream on that?" Djonny asked as he left for the fridge.

"It's on the third shelf back," Roxie said.

Just as Djonny got to the refrigerator door, it burst open and out popped Miss Orleans. She was wearing a long, sparkly gown and a sash over her shoulder. She did a slightly unpracticed fashion model step in her high-heeled shoes, taking the center aisle of the classroom like it was a runway. Her dress had barely enough open space below the knees to allow her legs to move.

"Didn't you just leave?" Djonny exclaimed, but he was ignored. Miss Orleans was far too busy controlling her step to answer. She was concentrating on not tumbling, keeping in motion while appearing to exert little effort in the process.

She was doing fine until the cameras began to flash. The Double Dog Dares entered the classroom with Kay leading the way, snapping photos of the beauty queen foods teacher.

The flashes blinded Miss Orleans and threw her off her controlled step. With no room to spread her knees to catch her balance, she nearly toppled over. Amazingly, she managed to keep herself upright, still moving forward.

She drew an earpiece from beneath her sash and plugged it in her ear as she moved. "They're here, Philip," she said to no one in the room. "I got them." And before the Double Dog Dares could make a break for it, they were surrounded by hall monitors.

"You're going to visit the principal," the head hall monitor told Kay. He pushed her unwillingly down the hall, and Miss Orleans followed, leaving her classroom once again.

Unsure of his sanity, Djonny looked to Roxie. She shrugged and said, "I guess it was a sting."

"Crazy," Djonny said. Warily, he opened the walk-in refrigerator door and called out. "Is there anyone else here?!"

When no one answered, he stepped inside, retrieved the cream, and brought it to Roxie. She proceeded to beat the cream, fluffing it with delicious air as Djonny sliced the pie into eight pieces. He pulled out two plates and put a piece of pie on each while Roxie added a friendly dollop of whipped cream.

With fork in hand, she tasted their creation. "Not bad. I'm usually my own worst critic, but this is really not bad." With that, she dove the fork back in for a second bite.

Djonny stuck a straw between his stitches and slurped noisily. "I like pie," he said. "Pie is good. But I like it best the way you make it."

22. Blades in Stereo

On his way out of the school, Djonny noticed students getting in step behind him. He wasn't sure what was going on, but he wanted to find out. First there were five, then ten, then twenty—all walking behind him. He knew they didn't all live in the same direction as him.

When Beto entered the lineup, Djonny stopped, turned, and approached him. "What's going on?"

Beto gave his usual arresting smile. "We know what you're going to do," he said. "We want to help, so we all decided to go with you."

"Where are you going with me . . . exactly?"

"You know. To the police department. To get Sam-O out."

"I didn't tell anyone. I only thought about it. How could all these people know what I was thinking?"

"I got *palabras*," Beto said. "Uh . . . how do you say it in English? Testes?"

Djonny blinked curiously. Beto must have meant "texts."

"Just say SMS," Djonny said, "if it's easier for you."

"Okay. I got SMS from Alicesteria saying she thought you were going to fight for Sam-O the same way you fought Mick and won."

"I'm glad you got your phone back," Djonny said. "So you and this Alicesteria . . . told the whole school . . . now they're all here to go and protest with me?"

"Man, you catch on fast."

"Who is she?"

"You met her this morning."

"I did?"

"Yes. Wavy blonde hair. Green eyes. She asked you about parties. You remember now?"

"Kind of, yeah. I thought her name was . . . Christy."

"Sometimes," Beto said, but before he could elaborate, the crowd began to grow restless.

A small group among the larger crowd began a chant: "Wrongly accused and abused! Wrongly accused and abused!"

"That's terrible! Stop!" Beto said before they could repeat it a third time. "We'll never get him out that way. They'll probably arrest *us*. How about something like: 'Sam-O, let 'im go!' That would be better."

A few near Beto tried the chant. It had a good rhythm and spread quickly. Djonny laughed at this turn. He was pleased with the others wanting to stand behind him in his cause, so he accepted their help by waving a hand over his head, signaling them to move. "Come on!" he said. "We have business with the sheriff!"

The students yelled in agreement and started walking again, with Djonny in the lead. Kevin wove his way through the crowd and found Djonny and Beto. Djonny felt invincible with his two best friends by his side and an army of chanters at his back.

The chanting teenage mob got many uncomfortable looks as they made their way through the city to the police station. Beto warned them before they got there to hold the chanting until they found out what was happening inside. If the police wouldn't let Sam-O free, then they would chant loud and long.

"Long?" some whispered. "How long?" It was evident some had not anticipated all the aspects of a true protest.

The police station was a clean building with nice, eco-friendly landscaping and not a few police cruisers parked in front. Inside was the standard extremely tall desk that made the officer in residence look down on you no matter how tall you were.

Djonny approached the desk and looked up. The mob behind him did not fit inside the lobby, so they stretched out through the glass double-doors and onto the plaza outside. They pushed forward, all wanting to hear what was being said.

The officer behind the too-tall desk glanced at Djonny, then at the mob. "Yes?" he said, making it clear he was talking to children. His hands were out of sight, and this made Djonny nervous.

Fortunately, Djonny could command his voice despite the nerves. He sang loudly, "Here for my friend . . . who was taken into custody today for crimes he did not commit."

"Uh huh," said the officer, still scanning the crowd. "And what . . ."

He stopped mid-sentence, looking past the crowd. Something was being set up on the plaza. A video camera. A news crew was there, preparing to film.

"He's innocent," Djonny said. "He didn't do it . . . just because he's a teenager . . ."

"Hold on now," the officer said. He climbed up onto the desk, spread his arms horizontally, bent his knees, and dove over Djonny's head into the middle of the mob.

The mob caught him, and the officer laughed. "Pass me outside!" he cried.

The mob complied, passing the policeman over their heads,

floating him on their hands, through the open doors to the plaza, where he leaned left and landed on his feet.

Djonny, Beto, and Kevin looked at each other, baffled. Then they did the only thing they could do under the circumstances. They reversed and went back outside.

The officer approached the news crew with his best public relations grin, all teeth and eyes. Djonny and his friends pushed their way through the gathered crowd as politely as they could, arriving in time to hear the officer feeding the news crew a line about ". . . nothing happening here other than a field trip for the local school."

"Is that your official statement?" Kevin asked, sounding sharp and political.

"This young man is not with the group," the officer said as the news crew continued setting up their equipment. Soon they had lights and sound, and one of their number, a young lady, said, "Recording live."

Djonny approached the news crew. "The group is with the group," he told them. "We're all here for the same reason. Our friend . . . he was wrongly accused."

The officer looked down at his shoes, beaten. The camera panned his way, and he perked up instantly, lighting his smile upon his face once again. "That may be true," he said, "but we can't technically let him out."

"Now?" one of the crowd asked Beto.

Beto nodded. "Now!"

"Sam-O, let 'im go! Sam-O, let 'im go! Sam-O, let 'im go!"

"I know," the officer began quietly, but his voice was drowned out.

The news crew tried to silence the crowd so they could hear what the officer was saying, but it was difficult to get a group of teenagers to settle once they were stirred up.

The officer continued, despite the noise of the chanting crowd. "I would like to let him go. I know he was falsely accused."

"Sam-O, let 'im go! Sam-O, let 'im go! Sam-O, let 'im go!"

Kevin, Beto, and Djonny held up their hands to silence the crowd, and the crowd obeyed.

What the officer said next made everyone's mind go fuzzy. "The young man who started the fire this morning also pulled the fire alarm this afternoon. He confessed. But we can't let Samuel Olson go because he's a juvenile. His parent or guardian has to come and

113

get him."

There was a general grumble from the mob, and several of them began leaving.

"Screw it," someone said.

"What was the use?" said another.

"Don't just give up," Djonny said. He turned to Kevin and Beto. "Do you have him on speed dial?"

"Yeah," Beto answered, "but we can't call him. He's locked up in there."

"Not what I meant."

"I got your meaning," Kevin said, sliding through his phone menus. "There! I got his mom's number and his dad's number."

"Do both," Djonny said urgently.

Kevin laughed behind his lips, dialed a number, and held the phone to his ear. After a short wait and brief hellos, he said, "Do you know where Sam-O is?" He read the TV channel emblem on the side of the camera. "Turn on Channel 2."

Immediately, he got an earful of frantic motherhood and decided to pass the phone on. "It's for you," he said, holding the phone out for the officer.

The officer took the phone reluctantly, saving his public relations smile. The voice on the other end of the phone was obviously not happy.

Beto slugged Kevin on the shoulder. "Smart to call his mom. His dad might have just said to keep him until he's eighteen."

Kevin laughed. "That's what my dad would have said."

The officer pushed the *End* button and passed the phone back to Kevin. Turning to the crowd but keeping his profile in view of the camera, he said, "His mother will be here in two minutes."

Cheers erupted from the crowd. Djonny jumped up and down with the rest of them but felt a little sad he couldn't shout with them. "We win!" he sang. "Oh, yeah! We'll *always* win!"

The officer was clearly pleased with the outcome and so gave a pleasant and truthful final statement to the news crew. Then he made his way quietly back inside the station.

The crowd waited patiently outside when Sam-O's mother came to get him. When the falsely accused came out, however, the partying began again. Cheering erupted from all sides. People ran up and hugged him. Djonny, Kevin, and Beto gave him fives, tens, and even twenties until Sam-O's palms were sore and his mom was tired of all the commotion and dragged him home.

Event over, the news crew packed their things
"A victory for the innocent!" Kevin exclaimed.
"That's not what his mom said," Djonny replied.
They all laughed and left, going their separate ways.

It had been a long day, and Djonny felt he had earned the right to trudge.

My right, he thought, *to live exactly how I want to live.*

On any other day on his way home from school, he *might* have trudged, but this day was different. He had been kissed by a crazy girl, stalked by her equally crazy boyfriend, won the battle, and in the final moments of school, had been kissed by a beautiful girl over a hot pie.

He decided not to trudge, but ran instead. He let the happy road fly beneath his feet. Arms pumped the air at his sides so that he was propelled forward like the deadly animal that he was. If there was prey before him, he was sure he would overtake it. He flew along cement and pavement and grass alike, nothing impeding his progress. Miles once vertical were knocked down horizontal so that the distance was soon eaten, beaten.

It felt like less than half a minute before he found the garden path, and he planted only one foot on the reconstituted cement to cover the distance. The familiar faces of animals in the hedges—the bantam, the coney, and the firefox—all flashed by as he ran to his house.

There too, in the garden, were the animal men: the toad-faced old man and his bird-like companion—the two strange men he had somehow attracted on the subway, and who had followed him home for no apparent reason. They were wet from head to toe.

Djonny considered their presence only briefly. They were needy, that was sure, but too dependent on their authority being universally understood. Djonny didn't even acknowledge it.

The toad-man raised a finger. "Just a moment, young man," he said, but Djonny flew past them, ignoring them both as easily as he'd done before.

He ran into the house and threw his jacket on a hook in the mudroom. He skip-slid in the kitchen when he realized he still had his boots on, so he spun and kicked the boots off his feet, launching them back into the mudroom.

Still energized and excited from the grand events of his day, Djonny ran up the stairs toward his room. The eerie blue light was still there, shining from underneath the mysterious door that had appeared that morning. Not wanting to awake whatever was in there, he tiptoed a wide circle around the door. The upper hallway felt strangely unfamiliar, as if it was not even a part of his house. The blue light leaking out from under the door made him feel like he'd stepped into a nauseous black-light party. The light reflected off the walls in gaudy purples, greens, even pinks, and projected an antiseptic (or was it pro-septic?) mood.

He went into his room and found nothing had been disturbed. Everything was in its place and familiar. Music came from his desktop, and he barely noticed the sounds. The music was as natural as birdsong in a forest, or horns in traffic.

Not so natural, however, was the state of his pet. One of the upper corners of the tank had been completely covered in webs. Within the thick, white webs was a dark shape. Inside the glass cage, no other creatures were present, not even a fly.

The shape inside the cocoon made a motion as his pet spider stretched its legs. They were pulling for some unknown reason, and Djonny leaned closer to see what was happening.

The black legs did their usual scratch dance, tapping the space ahead like a blind man's cane. As the legs found purchase within the web, they pulled. At first, it looked as if she was growing, but soon Djonny saw that she was leaving her midnight and blood-red skin behind. She slowly emerged from her cocoon, an albino version of her old self. Or so Djonny thought. Inspecting her more closely, he realized she was not white, but clear. Her clear carapace was showing him the color of the webs behind her.

As she pulled herself completely free of the chrysalis, Djonny also saw that she looked slimmer. She had left one other thing behind: an egg. The egg was not clear, but opaque. Though he couldn't see into it, he could see the shape of the egg change as tiny things moved inside, pressing outward at times, stretching the fabric of the egg to near translucence.

"What have you been doing in there?" he wanted to ask, but his lips were still seeled.

He remembered, too, that the music was no longer with him. He'd left his jacket on another level of the house. He looked at his mirror and saw the threads. Like Enola, he needed to come free of his cocoon, stretch out of his limiting shell.

Limiting, yes, he thought, *but without those limits, would I have gained so much?*

In just the space of a single day, he had discovered new friends, new forms of communication, and new ways to persuade an enemy. The threads were the catalyst to all of his discoveries—and he knew they had to go. He couldn't entertain the limits forever.

Still staring in the mirror, he regarded his bloodshot eyes with revulsion. He picked up his Redness Ender, the tiny dropper bottle with the claim "Stops eye spots" on the side. After only a drop in each eye, his whites began to clear.

Djonny found his scissors and brought them carefully up to his lips. He tried to remain steady, but the act of sliding even the dull edge of the blades along his lip, made him feel like he was going to sneeze. It was the same sensation he would get from staring at the sun on a dry summer day.

He pulled the scissors away, held them to the side, and sneezed. The spray patterned his mirror with hundreds of clear speckles.

"Oh, gross," he said from behind the threads.

He positioned the scissors again and got the same sensation, but now that he had let one out, he could control the urge better. With three snips, he had the threads unbound. Next, he pulled the threads through his skin. It was uncomfortable, though not as painful as he thought it might be. As he pulled the last thread through the sensitive flesh of his lips, he felt a sense of relief—as if a particular stage of life was over. Junior high, for instance.

Most humans in their right minds would feel relieved to have that stage over and done. Some, on the other hand—and there is always an "other" hand in life, as in the circus—would treasure fart jokes and uncomfortable, awkward innuendo for longer than maturity should normally allow.

Djonny didn't want to remain stuck in that immature place forever. He gathered up the black threads and threw them ceremonially in the trash. Looking back at the mirror, he practiced a few phrases.

"Hi, I'm Djonny," he said. "I'm . . . well, I *was* the deejay . . . for today."

It was his own voice, and certainly not as musical as the musicians whose voices he had borrowed all throughout that day. He could just as easily make up clever phrases with his own voice, but unfortunately, his voice was a sound he did not want to hear.

"I don't know what you can do about that, Djonny," he told his reflection.

"Keep talking, and get used to hearing yourself again," it replied.

"Right. I think you're right. There's no way around it, except to reacquaint—"

"Roxie has a good voice, doesn't she?"

"Are you kidding? She has a *great* voice."

"You won't talk to her, though. You're afraid."

"Afraid? Of what?"

"Rejection. Your own voice. Peer pressure."

"No way, not after today."

"You could still be rejected."

"But now I can talk. I can tell her exactly what's on my mind."

"Exactly, exactly. She was impressed by your jacket. What makes you think she would be as interested in plain Djonny the non-deejay?"

"Good point . . . I guess. Hey! Why are you trying to talk me out of it? I . . . you . . . we . . . have the same brain. The same body. We better agree on this, or—"

"Or we will be twice as rejected, right?" his reflection said.

"Right. And she's too amazing to lose."

"Whoa! Are you saying what I think you're saying?"

"Is she the one?"

He paused in the conversation, having forgotten which of these made-up characters was the negative side of his personality. Staring at himself didn't help solve the puzzle. It only made him think of someone else. Roxie. He was really too young to be contemplating eternity. He had other things to consider first. Like Roxie herself had said, "What are you going to do when you grow up?"

"What are you going to do?" he asked himself.

Then slowly, gradually, his mouth slid outward on both sides into a superior, all-knowing grin.

"Grin to win," he told himself. "And make their heads spin."

23. Once Upon a Fish

At the kitchen table that night, Djonny related all that had happened.

To their credit, his parents listened patiently and sweetly, even if many of the things Djonny had to say sounded impossible and contrived.

"It all started at Virgil's Modified Pet Store," Djonny said, as indeed it had. He told them about the purchase of the black widow spider, Enola, but skipped the details about the death of Penumbra and the appearance of the cocoon.

Djonny also told them about the trip on the subway. "—and there were these baseball players, and some kids dressed, or made up with makeup, like clowns. But that happened before I brought the spider home and after I had my lips sewn shut."

"Why did you do that?" Djonny's dad prompted.

"In honor of the homeless who never eat," Djonny replied, knowing his answer was farfetched but having no rational explanation He caught himself thinking in lyrics again, and almost said, "With no shoes on their feet . . . a pillow of concrete . . . with a smile incomplete . . . 'cause they're missing some teeth."

Instead, since his parents seemed to accept this explanation, he continued with his story. When he told them he'd been late for school, they exchanged a look that meant something, though the meaning was lost on Djonny. Behind their curious faces where Djonny could not see, they thought today was Saturday and wondered why he would go to school at all.

"I thought I was late, but I got there before the final bell."

"How did you get there?" Djonny's mom asked. "I didn't take you. I usually drive you."

Djonny thought about it for a moment but couldn't find the answer. He looked back and forth between his mom and dad. "I don't remember how I got there. Did I take the subway again?"

"Never mind," said his dad, "it doesn't matter now. You made it there, right? So what happened next?"

"Um, well, all the kids liked my jacket. I played music all day long. That's how I spoke: through music, and sometimes I played music to entertain people. In French class, all the girls were crazy about dancing. I was their deejay. So that was more fun than the usual lesson. Oh yeah, I almost forgot. This one kid challenged me to fight after school, but we never did. He backed out before the last period. He was crazy, though. He followed me around school all day, or so I heard. He sent me messages, thumb mail, and he even got one of my friends arrested."

Dad snorted. "Really?"

"Yeah. Just to get at me, you know, to get under my skin. He pulled the fire alarm, or he had someone do it. Actually, I don't know who pulled the fire alarm. I was in class with Noah and Isaiah. At least I was until I burned my fingers—"

"You did?" Mom interrupted. "You poor thing. Which ones?"

Djonny held his hands out to his mom. She looked them over, tops and bottoms. "They look okay," she pronounced.

"Well, I did get some ice on them pretty quick."

"Oh, that's good."

"Yeah, and while I was in lunch, this one kid slapped the back of my head. I almost swallowed my straw whole. I can't imagine trying to *digest* that. Anyway, he and I were friends by the end of the day." Djonny raised his eyebrows slyly. "So were Roxie and I. She even gave me her number so I can call her later."

"Roxie, huh?" Dad asked. "Is she cute?"

"Not cute," Djonny said and shook his head, "...foxy."

"Oh-ho, foxy, is she? I don't remember any girls in my junior high school being foxy."

"Yeah, she's amazing, but she never really noticed me before today. I think it was the music that got her attention. That, and I helped her out of a little—problem."

"What was that?"

"I just loaned her my jacket for a class. She was grateful, I think. Actually, come to think of it, she never did say thanks. Not verbally, anyway. The people who talk usually talk too much, and the ones you wish would talk don't. You know? Like that Rascler kid. He came up to me begging for change, but the only change I gave him was a change of scenery. The way he jingled, it sounded like he didn't need anything anyway. And Jill Renee was there. She's pretty much the funniest person in our whole school. She made the other kids laugh at me, but she didn't mean to do it. They just didn't know what I was thinking at the time. It turned out fine, so no harm done. I asked her a riddle, and she answered it better than anyone ever has."

"Is she foxy too?" Dad wanted to know, and Mom slugged him on the shoulder to let him know what she thought about the question.

"Well, I don't think so, but she is pretty. Probably somebody thinks she's foxy."

"And if you're foxy," Dad said, grabbing Mom around the waist and pulling her close, "I'm comin' to get ya."

"For electronics class, I got to make my own computer," Djonny said to distract himself from his parents' affection. "I built it myself. Then, in programming, I got to build the operating system and the rest of the software. I put some music on it and some videos from the other guys in the class. Oh, and one of the guys in shop class lost a finger. That was seriously gross. But they took him to the hospital to have it sewn back on."

"Wow, sounds like you had a full day," Dad said.

"I did. The best part was the end, but that's how school always is, isn't it? Beto and I did a circuit training in gym class, and everything after that was much better. He danced all the girls down the hallway at the end of the day. Before that, there was a fire in the bathroom on level three, but it got put out by the fire sprinklers with a little help from Darrel, not to mention the long-haired rockers, and everything was okay after that. Oh, but one wing of the building was so old it collapsed. No one was in it at the time."

"Holy crash, Batman, did anything *not* happen at your school today?" Mom asked.

"One of the teachers died, too, but I'm not sure that happened today. We had a moment of silence for her. At least they requested a moment of silence. Some of the kids were a little loud about how glad they were that she was dead. She was really old."

"I hope *you* were respectful," Mom said.

"Well, sure, it was easy for me. I never took one of her classes."

"Djooonny," Mom reprimanded him.

"There is this one teacher who gets on my nerves. He's always insinuating things about me. Today, a kid asked me if I wanted to go get high, and I pretty much told him no way, but the teacher acted like this kid and I were best friends, chumming it up and all that. I don't get it. He has mental problems or something."

"Yeah," Dad agreed, "some people are like that. I don't think there's anything you can do except limit your time around that person. If it was a job, I'd say, 'Don't work with that guy.'"

From the kitchen there came the light sound of a bell. For a moment, Djonny tried to think which class he was supposed to go to next. Then Mom got up, saving his sanity. "Dinner's ready."

"What is it tonight, dear?"

"Wait and see."

Dad stared at Djonny with nervous calculation in his eyes. "I do love her cooking, but why does it always have to be a surprise?"

Mom returned with a tray of legs. The rest of the animal was mysteriously not present. "Frog legs," she announced, though it was unnecessary. Her two men could see what was on the tray.

Dad rubbed his hands together excitedly and made a low rumble behind his closed lips. "Mmmmmmm . . . I'll have four . . . teen."

Djonny, on the other hand, declined. "There's just something unsettling about the fact that a fish grew legs," he said. "I don't think I can do it right now, Mom. Sorry."

She nodded understandingly and passed him a roll.

10. The Sirkus (Epilog)

Djonny had been loitering too long at the drinking fountain on the first floor. Before he had a chance to get his liquid for the day, the same clown-faced boys from the subway cornered him, grabbed him from all sides, and thrust him in a locker.

It was dark as a sinner's soul in there. Through the locker door, he heard the clowns laughing and chanting, "Locker number forty-five, no one gets out alive. Locker number forty-five, no one gets out alive. Locker number forty-five, no one gets out alive."

The sound diminished as the clowns moved along to bother someone else. He knew they weren't going to come back and let him out.

As Djonny stood in the tall, narrow space feeling lonely and abandoned, he began to hear sounds coming from deeper in the locker. They were voices. They began as whispers at first, some growing louder as others fell like a tide. Djonny imagined he was hearing ghostly voices from the other side of the thin veil separating the living from the dead.

Momentarily, he also imagined he saw lights in the back of the locker, but he knew this couldn't be so. The lockers had metal backs, and those backs backed onto a brick wall. There couldn't be lights there.

He reached a hand toward the light and felt cloth. Cloth? Moving closer, he heard the metallic clattering of clothes hangers. There was depth to the locker after all.

He took another small step and found himself encircled in hanging clothes. With a thrust of his arms, he opened a space to see beyond the darkness and confinement. What he saw there was fun and excitement: There was a dunk tank with a large gal seated atop the plank.

"Won't somebody dunk me?" she said, her voice melancholy and sweet.

A spotlight landed on Djonny, and he heard applause. He looked in the direction of the sound and found the waving motion of an ocean of heads—an audience in the dim recess surrounding a central circle of light. He stepped forward, bringing himself dizzily into the center of that circle of light.

The floor was made of earth; earth that had been trampled down by large animals. Horses, probably, and elephants, too—or rhinoceri, maybe. There was a man juggling knives at the periphery of the circle. He smiled at Djonny as if they were old friends and caught the knives. He motioned to Djonny with one hand as if to get him started doing something.

"Oh," Djonny almost said, but the threads binding his lips prevented him.

He shook his head at his forgetfulness and keyed up some circus music.

"Here, ladies and gentlemen, is the greatest juggler of knives in the universe!" Djonny said, using his device to create a harmonic blend of music and words. It was quite a bit trickier with his handheld than it would have been with his desktop at home, but he made it work.

A spotlight landed on the juggler. The knives flew and spun, catching the light beautifully, glinting and reflecting the spotlight in such a way that the audience became a speckled field of smiling faces. This juggler really was the best. He caught one knife in his teeth and continued to juggle the rest. He then began to add knives from behind his back to the arc—ten, twenty, thirty!

Thirty knives spun gracefully in the air above the juggler's head. The circus music came to an end. The crowd fell silent, as if all who witnessed were expecting the juggler to stab himself, or lose a limb.

The juggler spat out the knife that was in his mouth and began talking, still maintaining the illusion of weightlessness in the knives. He chuckled loudly to relieve the tension. "Don't worry," he told the crowd, "I've practiced this trick two times before . . ."

The audience laughed nervously, not yet ready to release their collective tension.

"What I am about to try, however, I have never done before. Not even in practice." The juggler straightened his posture and shifted his arc of blades to the right two steps. "Djonny," he said, "do you think you could catch some of these for me?"

Wisely, Djonny said, "I only deejay . . . and right now, emcee."

Then, to show the crowd exactly what he meant, Djonny played a manic song that sounded like a brass band falling down and getting back up, then falling down again.

The juggler looked upset, and Djonny wondered if his musical choice had been a mistake. But then the juggler smiled at Djonny, reassuring him that it was all an act, and called out to his assistant instead. "Theresa! Will you help me, please?"

A beautifully plump woman in a sparkly tutu, tights, and a puffy white shirt emerged from the shadows. She smiled broadly, showing off a perfect set of teeth framed by a brightly painted pair of lips—red over white.

Theresa marched forward and took a position facing the juggler. "Okay, Paul," she said. "I'm ready!"

Djonny amped up the music to excite the crowd, but the juggler, Paul, said, "Not yet! First, we have to blindfold each other."

With a wicked grin, Paul retrieved two long strips of cloth from his pocket. Between knives, he threw the blindfolds at Theresa. "Here you go. You get the honors."

She caught them gracefully and moved behind Paul to tie a strip of cloth around his eyes. He didn't miss a beat, keeping the rhythm of the knives going like his own personal collection of deadly pet butterflies. He didn't even lose the rhythm when Theresa gave the knot on the back of his head a violent tug to make it super-tight.

Laughing, Theresa gave a showbusiness twirl and held up her own blindfold for all to see. Daintily, she covered her eyes with the cloth, finishing it off with a loose knot to the side of her head.

"Are you prepared for this, Theresa?" the juggler asked dramatically, as if she couldn't possibly be prepared and was surely going to be sent to her doom.

The crowd was not oblivious to this, and some of the women in the audience gasped. A murmur broke out among the light-speckled crowd, and Theresa held up her hands in the universal gesture for silence. She wanted them all to know that she was, indeed, prepared.

"Throw the knives, Paul. I'm ready."

She didn't even catch the first knife. It flew past her blindfolded face and rolled in the dirt. Voices in the crowd were growing concerned, but Theresa silenced them again with her raised hands.

Before the next knife came, she pulled the blindfold down from her eyes and rested it around her neck like a fashionable scarf. She turned her head to the audience and gave a conspiratorial wink, letting them be part of her plan. Then, as the next knife flew toward the back of her head aiming to kill her, she spun and caught it with a swift, practiced hand. The knife flew from her hand to the dirt floor, stabbing it with a wet *thunk*.

Theresa brought her act to climax by holding her forearm to her forehead and putting a hand over her heart. She then screamed the most violent horror-show scream. "You've killed me, Paul! I'm surely dead!"

Despite her words, the juggler kept throwing the knives and even increased their frequency. Theresa caught them and stabbed them in the dirt as before, at every third knife letting out a horrible scream that shook the emotions of all who heard.

It was apparent to Djonny why this woman had been hired to do what she did. Her scream was as piercing as a sharp knife. She could scream with the best of them, all the while catching flying knives, even if it was only one at a time. Her movements were like a flamenco dance, with a sharp, clipped step and the knives thrown behind in snapping thrusts. Her smile never wavered, so that even when she screamed, she had a bright smile for the hypnotized audience.

As the thirtieth knife was planted in the dirt, Paul's hands continued moving, searching for the next falling blade.

"That's the last one!" Theresa shouted.

127

Paul pulled his blindfold up with caution. He spied his assistant, intact and unharmed. He spied the crowd, entertained and fascinated. All as hoped. All as practiced and planned.

Taking the cue, Djonny exclaimed, "Juggler of knives! Paul! The greatest juggler in the universe!"

Paul took a bow, then another as the crowd cheered. "Encore!" they shouted, so Paul took a third bow, remained in that bent position, and pulled the knives from the dirt only to begin juggling them again. Theresa helped gather, but Djonny didn't let her get away.

"Let's give a hand to Theresa!" he told the crowd.

Most of the audience clapped, but a couple of men jumped out of the stands and took Djonny's words literally, helping Theresa pull knives like carrots out of the dirt, insisting on carrying the ones she had already secured.

Theresa shrugged and gave them over, which freed her up to take a bow. As she did, the crowd went wild, many of them trying to mimic her scream. Most were less than sincere, weary attempts, so Theresa showed them how it was done—belting out a scream to rock the house. The men with armloads of knives were most impressed. One whistled, and another hollered, "Wow! What a set of pipes!"

As Paul and Theresa exited the ring, a line of elephants made their way in, trumpeting and nearly scaring the pants off the helpful men. The assistant's assistants dropped their knives and ran back to their places in the audience.

Right as the elephants were trotting out, Djonny caught sight of a tiny caterpillar doing its arched walk toward him. It had an interesting metallic glitter on or near its face, and Djonny thought he heard it say, "My turn." But the elephants were very loud, and they drowned out his voice. Djonny watched in horror as one of the elephants stepped on the caterpillar, smashing it to a pulp.

Too late for that one, Djonny thought and launched into an improvisational introduction for the elephants. "And here is our next act, the elephants—"

An elephant trainer arrived carrying a large carved staff. "We're the Fiery Flying Elephants," he said quietly to Djonny.

"Ladies and gentlemen!" Djonny announced, swinging into it. "Here, I give you the FIERY FLYING ELEPHANTS!"

Six elephants circled Djonny, and it was no irony that he felt incredibly small, like a caterpillar about to be squashed. The ground shook with the trotting tonnage. The trainer guided the elephants inside the circle, near Djonny. With the passing of each elephant, the trainer signaled so that each in turn trumpeted.

When all had trumpeted, the trainer stopped and held the staff directly in front of him with two hands. He paused to watch that all of the elephants had ceased trotting. Satisfied, he began spinning the staff like a propeller.

Three of the six elephants sat down in the dirt, and from there they rolled over onto their backs, feet up in the air. The other three slowly climbed onto the upturned feet of those on their backs. Once balanced, the three higher elephants curled into balls, and the elephants holding them up began to spin them, playing with them like beach balls.

The trainer leaned in close to Djonny. "In practice, they often drop one another," he said. "But they won't do it here in front of people."

"Is it loud?" Donny couldn't help asking.

The trainer nodded. "Enough to make you think of a small earthquake."

As long as the trainer's staff spun, the elephants twirled in the air like playful children. He slowed his staff, letting it slip through his grasp until the base touched the earthen floor. Moving in sync with the staff, the lower elephants let the flying elephants descend slowly. When they were finally on the ground, the elephants began a synchronized wobbling step that made them look gracefully dizzy.

Djonny didn't know if it was part of the act and moved with them in a circling motion.

The elephant trainer leaned in close and whispered, "Our next feat is the fiery portion of our act," prompting Djonny to dutifully announce: "And now, for your enjoyment and pleasure—!"

A group of elephant trainers emerged from the shadows carrying buckets of liquid. They were dressed just like the trainer but were much hairier, resembling chimpanzees in costumes. They set the buckets down in front of the elephants and waited. As the trainer lifted his staff and brought it down in a repeating motion, the elephants dunked their trunks in the buckets. Then they lifted their trunks and sprayed the air. The chimp trainers raised their staffs to the spray and ignited it, filling the air above with gigantic bursts of flame.

Soon, the elephants were doing a choreographed routine in time with the flame bursts. The flames grew smaller, changing color, shifting from red to white.

Djonny matched the flame bursts with a piece of music that bass-lined at the moment of ignition. As he performed his DJ duties, he looked out into the crowd and recognized the toad-faced man and his bird-faced partner watching. They worked their way to the front row, shoving onlookers aside, and although most of the crowd appeared upset, they were too frightened to do anything about it. The birdman did a slow nod, and the people settled elsewhere.

The fire sprayed over the audience's heads, riveting their attention. Meanwhile, a group of six men came out and covertly changed the buckets. The fires were small and blue now, and the elephants were dancing less flamboyantly.

Suddenly, the elephants flew into a rage. They bounded wildly before their trainer and his chimpanzee impostors, and one of the chimps was engulfed in blue flame. He ran outside the circle of elephants, flames trailing off his head. A few people in the crowd told him to roll, but it was possible he had no concept of the word.

Djonny looked at the dunk tank and got an idea. He ran to the toad-like man and boldly reached into his suit pocket, retrieving the baseball the man had stolen on the train that morning. Djonny raised the ball and took aim.

The elephants danced defiantly as the trainers commanded them to be calm, trumpeting loudly and flailing their trunks. Djonny threw the baseball, and it connected with the center of the dunk tank target. Before the audience could fathom what was happening, the elephants lined up, thrust their trunks into their buckets, and proceeded to spray the audience, soaking them. The baseball tripped the dunk tank plank, and the large gal fell excitedly into the water. A giant wave splashed out, dowsing the frying chimp, who fell in an exhausted heap.

With a raised baton, the trainer got the elephants in order. Once again, the elephants danced, this time with coordination, and once again they dunked their trunks and sprayed the audience. Realizing it was only water, the audience welcomed the pleasant mist.

The trainer winked at Djonny, so Djonny polled the audience. "Is everything cool?!"

His question was answered by cheers and loud whistles. Apparently, they loved it. To this clamor, the elephants took their bows, bending their front legs and laying trunks in the dirt. The chimpanzees bowed with them and led the elephants out through the center ring's exit.

As soon as the elephants were out, there came a thunderclap, and a thick, black cloud formed in the center of the ring. Not wanting to breathe it in, Djonny took four quick steps to the outer edge of the ring. Within the smoke, he saw the image of a man. The man was wearing a cloak and carrying a trident taller than he was. By the shadow of the smoke, it looked as if the man was growing horns out of his head.

Djonny's face clouded in concern. "Have I been that bad?" he asked.

The horned man stepped from the cloud, waving the smoke away from his face. He smiled at the crowd, pulled the band with the horns off of his head, and threw them into the assembly. Audience members tried to get their hands on the souvenir, and there came a minor wrestling match. A large man rose from the melee with the horns and promptly gave them to his son.

The performer, now hornless, shed his cloak, though he did not throw it to the crowd. He instead threw the gaudy, red velvet thing to the ground, revealing a pair of red boots, red pants, and red suspenders. The thick tuft of hair on his chest might have been considered clothing—a hair-shirt, if one chose to think of it that way. As for the trident, he planted that at his feet in the dirt.

His hands waved, moving passionately, expertly in the air. He threw his hands upward like a man summoning the demon he had recently pretended to be, or perhaps a man coaxing wilder sounds from an orchestra. The cloak at his feet began to rise, bouncing and tugging upward, filling itself out with a life of its own. Then, beneath the cloak, the audience saw feet. They were the furry feet of a tiger.

Djonny took one more step away and found himself at the low wall that defined the edge of the performance ring. He wondered at the tameness of the magician's pet. He wondered if he should start for the exit now or wait to see what was next in the routine. Of course, seeing a tiger up close with no cage between was far from routine.

Now I know how the mouse feels, he thought.

Once the tiger was fully materialized, the magician whipped the cloak from off the top of the large cat. The tiger roared, letting everyone know who was the strongest under the big tent. Not a one of the humans present dared to disagree.

The magician reached behind his back and produced a ball of red yarn. Finding the loose end, he threw the ball at the tiger's face while holding the end so as to let a length of it play out. The ball of yarn hit the tiger square in the face, bounced, and almost hit the dirt, but

131

the tiger was too fast and pounced on it before it could land. The tiger then wrestled with the yarn, fully occupied.

The magician beckoned Djonny closer, but Djonny refused, shaking his head and maintaining his place at the wall. The magician put on a face of disappointment and impatience. He snapped his fingers, and Djonny's device began to play a magical tune complete with tinkling cymbals and deep brass horns. He stared at his device, amazed. This was one tricky magician.

The magician stepped over the large cat, which was busy slobbering all over the ball of yarn and passing it from paw to paw. On the other side of the tiger, the magician pulled his suspenders away from his chest and let them snap back. He then held his hands out in front of him and squatted slowly. He stared at the crowd viciously, stood up swiftly, and did a spin turn. As he spun, he disappeared.

Djonny's music stopped. There was tense silence as everyone looked at the tiger, wondering how long it would remain entertained by the yarn. Its feline teeth were apparent as it gnawed at the ball, and its claws were extended fully, as large and sharp as the jungle would allow.

The silence was disrupted when Djonny's device magically announced, "Whoever wants to take my trident home can have it. My cloak, too. And anyone desiring the biggest jungle cat souvenir is welcome to have it. Be warned, though. He eats way too much."

No one moved. Another tense silence weighed tangibly over the crowd. When the silence had reached its heaviest, the voice returned. "Don't sweat it. I was just kidding."

With that announcement, the tiger went out the way the magician had come in: in a thunderclap and a thick cloud of smoke. When the smoke dissipated and the tiger was seen to be truly gone, the crowd sighed in relief. Nervous chatter filled the spaces in and between all who came to be spectators of the awe and magic of the circus. Djonny played a playful, gentle tune to relieve the tension. The magician came trotting out from the performers' area to the sound of a few laughs. He waved at the crowd, grabbed his trident and cloak, and returned the way he came.

The freak show was next. The first of the performers was a man swinging twenty-pound weights from his ears. "We're the freak show," he told Djonny. "Tell them to not fear the freaks." Behind him was a woman with her beard braided in reverse rainbow-colored strings—red at her chin and purple near her navel. She wore the clothing of a belly dancer and had the moves to match. Her spangles shook as she approached.

Djonny snapped himself out of his daze and announced the procession. "Have no fear! Freaks on parade!"

The next woman, a dwarf, corrected him. "Not my children. They're normal."

Behind the dwarf came a giant of a man, his head such a tall mass of flesh and bone that it was evident he needed his large body to carry that cranium around. His entire head grinned.

In answer to Djonny's unasked question—"I wonder if this is the dwarf lady's child?"—the giant said, "Not me. Them," and pointed a massive thumb behind him. "I'm the husband," he added in a booming bass voice.

Trailing the dwarf and the giant were three extra-normal people. Djonny guessed they were in their twenties. They were dressed in jeans and polo shirts with sweaters tied around their waists or shoulders. Of average height, they were as standard as could be, and surprisingly, they were the ones who received a distasteful murmur from the audience.

Is it that the normal ones shouldn't be in the parade of freaks? Djonny wondered. *Or is it that the normal ones are the freakiest of all?*

A wolfboy came out on all fours next, racing past Djonny and startling him out of his interior questioning. The wolfboy wore pants and a jacket, but his shoes were his own hairy feet. They matched the incredibly hairy hands on which he clawed his way across the dirt floor.

Not far behind him came a girl carrying an A-frame X-ray. The X-ray clearly displayed her bones, from her ribs down to her femurs, and most in the audience thought it was not so freakish as amazing to see her bones in motion.

As she walked past Djonny, she let out a little squeak, and Djonny realized it was gas. She blushed and whispered, "Excuse me."

"Hey," Djonny said playfully, "I saw that."

The X-ray girl turned a deep shade of red. "You did?"

"No!" Djonny said, waving her on. "Just kidding."

As the X-ray girl hurriedly chased after the wolfboy, there came a set of twins of the closest kind. Sharing a hipbone, they walked with four legs and waved to the audience with four arms. Both were male and shared the modified accouterments of a business suit.

Each had his own style of mustache: one favored the waxed, thin, curled variety; the other grew his fat and bushy and wore glasses and a top hat.

As they stopped before Djonny, the twin with the top hat and glasses asked, "Do you mind if I take over for a moment?"

"Emcee?"

"Precisely," said the twin, sounding like a gentleman from the old country.

"Be my guest," Djonny said.

The twins held up their hands. As they did, black-and-white batons appeared in their hands. They spun them in a synchronized twirl as the top hat twin began his monolog.

"And now, for your extreme pleasure, ladies and gents, we have another magic show. It is the participatory style for you now, so we shall require two or three of you to come out here and be part of the show."

As expected, many hands were raised. The twins made a show of selecting their volunteers. They walked back and forth, giving the audience a moment of suspense as the twin in the top hat spoke. "We will need someone who is strong enough to handle our sort of magic. Also, someone who is not afraid of . . . of anything, really!"

To his surprise, Djonny saw the three clown-faced boys who had tormented him on the subway earlier and more recently shoved him in the locker. How they had arrived here was a mystery, but here they were, standing in the front row, waving their hands high and hollering, "Pick us! We're not afraid of anything!"

After passing them by twice, the twin with the top hat finally pointed his baton at them. "You three are decorated as if you belong in the circus! We may as well have you out here with us."

With that, the three clown-faced boys leapt over the low wall to the ring. Djonny suppressed his dislike of them having been chosen, saying nothing out of respect for the twins.

Meanwhile, the stage folks made themselves busy sneaking props out to the ring. There was a cannon, large and ominous in the center, and on either side of it, a wheel of death and a saw table.

"Very well, then," the top hat twin said to the clown-faced boys. "Who wants to be shot and who wants to be cut?"

The boys grew suddenly timid. They huddled together at the side of the ring, none wanting to volunteer now, none wanting to exclaim their strength or lack of fear.

"You know I'm joking, of course!" the top hat twin said. "We are magicians. There is not an ounce of pain in this kind of shooting and cutting. We shall do it with style and grace." He pointed at the boy with the smeared eye paint. "You shall go first. Up to the table with you!"

The twins showed their strength as they forced the less-than-willing clown to the saw table, picking him up and putting him in the box. To his credit, he did not protest, not even when they closed the box around him so that his arms, legs, and head stuck out. The only expression he showed was the uncomfortable grimace of torment.

The twins spun the box for the pleasure of the audience. The box was not attached to the table, and when it was done spinning, the clown's head was pointing the opposite direction. He was in there, for sure.

Each ditched his baton in trade for a large metallic saw. Because there were two saws, the twins could cut in two places at once, and they stretched and bowed the saws above their heads, finally snapping them into place in the slits at the top of the box.

The clown in the box giggled nervously. Holding the box with their free hands (their center hands), the twins cut through rapidly, one right-handed, the other left. As they got to the point where the clown's body must have been, the boy began to scream. "Oh! Something's wrong! You're cutting me!"

Blood began pouring from the box, and that was when everyone decided the screaming was only part of the show. The other clown-faced boys were not so sure and were about to make a run for the exit when two strong men in leopard loincloths came up behind them and told them to stay put.

The screaming continued as the saws did their back-and-forth horror show, forcing more red liquid through the gaps in the box. It really seemed to be more fluid than could possibly be contained in one human.

When they were finished, the clown-faced boy lay still and silent. The twins zipped their saws free of the box and took a quick bow as the saw table and its cargo were removed from the ring.

The twins gestured for the next clown, the boy with the long black frown painted over his mouth, to take his place on the wheel of death. His painted frown was elongated by the real frown on his lips. Finding himself between the wall of musclebound men and the terrifying twins, he obediently walked to his doom.

They strapped him in, and the twin with the waxed mustache

said, "Please don't struggle. If you're thrashing about, it is very difficult not to strike you with the throwing knives."

The boy's eyes went wide, and his face drew slack in shock. The waxed-mustache twin took up a handful of throwing knives. Once he was ready, he nodded, the wheel was spun, and the throwing began.

He threw one, and it whizzed past the wheel.

"Whoa!" cried the spinning clown. It was not apparent if he was relieved or amazed.

The twins held up four hands, and the wheel was halted. They turned to the audience. "Don't you think we should blindfold him?" the top hat twin said, and the crowd went wild in agreement.

To the crowd's extreme pleasure, Theresa returned carrying a blindfold. The wheel had been stopped upside down, so Theresa spun it a half-turn and brought it upright. She put the blindfold over the boy's eyes as tightly as she could, gave the wheel a merciless spin, laughed, and skipped back to stand beside the twins.

Craning his neck to address the crowd, the top hat twin said, "Now I'm going to try it by a different method. I almost never miss the target when I do it this way."

To everyone's surprise, Theresa threw the next knife. It struck the wheel of death and buried into the wood no more than an inch from the clown-faced boy's ear.

"Whoa!" he cried again, his voice high-pitched and fearful. "That was too close!"

Theresa wound her arm up and threw again. This time, the knife struck the wood near the clown's leg. The audience cheered, and Theresa seemed to grow more confident with their backing.

She held her hands palms out, and the top hat twin said, "Silence!"

When the audience was sufficiently quiet, Theresa stood post-like, meditating for her final throw. The twins got ready too, picking up several knives and holding them out for her skilled fingers.

Theresa finished her meditation and began whirling about, snatching up knives, hurling them as fast as she could pick them up. The knives pelted the wheel like a lethal hail of steel. Two of the knives hit the wheel on their sides and bounced away into the darkness beyond the spotlights, but the rest of them stabbed their target—right down to the very last one, which pierced the clown right in the center of the blindfold.

Theresa and the twins were too busy giving knuckles and fives to notice the blood gushing from the silent clown's head. His blood mixed with his black face paint, turning his frown purple. The stagehands unpinned him from the wheel and carried him out of the ring and out of the light. He disappeared out there, somewhere beyond the arena, beyond the show.

Done with the congratulatory hand slapping, Theresa made her way from the ring, trotting playfully out of the lights.

Now it was down to the last clown. Djonny knew him as Rob, the boy with lightning bolts drawn over his eyes. By his fidgety stance, it seemed Rob wanted to bolt like lightning, but he was trapped as the others had been.

Although the audience clearly thought it was a good show, Rob did not. He tried showing them his angry face to no effect, and ramming his head against the ultra-tough abdomen of one of the loincloth-clad strong men was as fruitless.

As a last-ditch effort, he tried denial: "I didn't really want to be here. My friends made me!"

Down to his last straw, Rob tried bargaining. "I don't want to die," he pleaded. "I'll do anything you want. I'll help you bring down the circus tents. I'll follow the elephants around with a bucket and a shovel. Anything! Please, don't make me!"

The twins laughed maniacally and replied in unison. "We're going to make you! Make you! Make you!"

Their chant caught on with the audience, who repeated it and stomped their feet as they clapped their hands. "Make you! Make you! Make you!"

Djonny replayed the twins' words over the loudspeakers so that he was easily as loud as the gathered crowd, if not louder.

While all of this was going on, the twins quietly told Rob that the quickest way to get out of the circus was to climb into the cannon so they could shoot him out. He complied grudgingly, his lightning eyeshadow looking rather appropriate when his face poked out of the cannon's end.

Rob's expression took on a comical blend of constipation and dread not hidden by his face paint. The moment he smelled the burning fuse, his expression changed to baby tears. He howled like a beagle, but not for long. With a boom and spark, the last of the clown-faced boys exited the arena—through the top of the tent.

"Oops!" the top hat twin said mischievously, "we forgot to open the flap."

The crowd went wild, stomping and shouting louder than they

had for anything else.

"And now we're done," the top hat twin announced as he and his brother pushed the cannon out of the ring.

The first magician came back and took a bow, as did one of the elephants and the head trainer. Others followed quickly, including Paul, the juggler, and Theresa, who received a massive round of applause. The freak show received a standing ovation, and the twins returned for one final bow. The spotlights went out; the audience followed.

In the dim light, eyes still adjusting, Djonny said, "Does anyone have any idea how I can get . . . out of the darkened room . . . back to school?"

"Follow them," said one of the strong men, and he pushed Djonny toward the exodus of paying customers.

Djonny was thrust so hard that he ran into a man carrying a bag of peanuts, a mustard-covered hot dog, and a drink. The man shoved back, and Djonny wheeled backwards into the person behind him. People began jostling at him on all sides, and Djonny realized the situation was just like the hallways at school. With a start, he realized that was where he was: back at school amid the throngs of students.

He smiled, thinking it had to be some of the twins' special magic, but after a moment he realized he was truly back. He focused his intent on making his way through the mid-class migration. It was a jarring way to re-enter reality, but Djonny was glad to be back all the same.

About the Author

Kurt Gailey has an inner desire to one day become a genetic modification technician. His past and current careers include: chemist, electrician, and submariner. As a scientist, he has a natural curiosity that leaves him with more questions than answers.

"Why do authors write fictional novels in first person and then write autobiographical paragraphs in third person?"

"Why are botanists not 'botanologists'?"

"If a tomato is a fruit, why not put one in your ice cream?"

"Have you ever been so sick you hallucinated?"

"What would you do if you couldn't talk?"

Questions like these are what inspired *Sound Distortion*, a psychedelic sci-fi novel that is as entertaining as it is unusual.

About the Publisher

Glass Spider Publishing is an independent publisher located in Ogden, Utah. The company was founded in 2016 by writer Vince Font to help underrepresented authors gain visibility. For more information, visit www.glassspiderpublishing.com.

 GLASS**SPIDER**PUBLISHING